THE LAST TYCOON

BY F. SCOTT FITZGERALD

NOVELS

THE LAST TYCOON *(unfinished)*
with a foreword by Edmund Wilson and notes by the author
TENDER IS THE NIGHT
THE GREAT GATSBY
THE BEAUTIFUL AND DAMNED
THIS SIDE OF PARADISE

STORIES

BITS OF PARADISE
uncollected stories by Scott and Zelda Fitzgerald
THE BASIL AND JOSEPHINE STORIES
edited with an introduction by Jackson R. Bryer and John Kuehl
THE PAT HOBBY STORIES
with an introduction by Arnold Gingrich
TAPS AT REVEILLE
SIX TALES OF THE JAZZ AGE AND OTHER STORIES
with an introduction by Frances Fitzgerald Smith
FLAPPERS AND PHILOSOPHERS
with an introduction by Arthur Mizener
THE STORIES OF F. SCOTT FITZGERALD
a selection of 28 stories, with an introduction by Malcolm Cowley
BABYLON REVISITED AND OTHER STORIES

STORIES AND ESSAYS

AFTERNOON OF AN AUTHOR
with an introduction and notes by Arthur Mizener
THE FITZGERALD READER
with an introduction by Arthur Mizener

LETTERS

THE LETTERS OF F. SCOTT FITZGERALD
with an introduction by Andrew Turnbull
LETTERS TO HIS DAUGHTER
with an introduction by Frances Fitzgerald Smith
DEAR SCOTT/DEAR MAX
edited by John Kuehl and Jackson Bryer

AND A COMEDY

THE VEGETABLE
with an introduction by Charles Scribner III

THE

LAST TYCOON

an unfinished novel

by

F. SCOTT FITZGERALD

A CHARLES SCRIBNER'S SONS BOOK
MACMILLAN PUBLISHING COMPANY
NEW YORK

Charles Scribner's Sons
Macmillan Publishing Company
866 Third Avenue, New York, NY 10022
Collier Macmillan Canada, Inc.

ISBN 0-684-15311-4

Macmillan books are available at special discounts for bulk purchases for sales
promotions, premiums, fund-raising, or educational use.

For details, contact:
Special Sales Director
Macmillan Publishing Company
866 Third Avenue
New York, NY 10022

First Scribner / Macmillan Hudson River Edition 1988

10   9   8   7   6   5

Printed in the United States of America

FOREWORD

Scott Fitzgerald died suddenly of a heart attack (December 21, 1940) the day after he had written the first episode of Chapter 6 of his novel. The text which is given here is a draft made by the author after considerable rewriting; but it is by no means a finished version. In the margins of almost every one of the episodes, Fitzgerald had written comments—a few of them are included in the notes—which expressed his dissatisfaction with them or indicated his ideas about revising them. His intention was to produce a novel as concentrated and as carefully constructed as *The Great Gatsby* had been, and he would unquestionably have sharpened the effect of most of these scenes as we have them by cutting and by heightening of color. He had originally planned that the novel should be about 60,000 words long, but he had written at the time of his death about 70,000 words without, as will be seen from his outline, having told much more than half his story. He had calculated, when he began, on leaving himself a margin of 10,000 words for cutting; but it seems certain that the novel would have run longer than the proposed 60,000 words. The subject was here more complex than it had been in *The Great Gatsby*—the picture of the Hollywood studios required more space for its presentation than the background of the drinking life of Long Island; and the characters needed more room for their development.

This draft of *The Last Tycoon*, then, represents that point in the artist's work where he has assembled and organized his material and acquired a firm grasp of his theme, but has not yet brought it finally into focus. It is remarkable that, under these circumstances, the story should have already so much power and the character of Stahr emerge with so much intensity and reality. This Hollywood producer, in his misery and grandeur, is certainly the one of Fitzgerald's central figures which he had thought out most completely and which he had most deeply come to understand. His notes on the character show how he had lived with it over a period of three years or more, filling in Stahr's idiosyncrasies and tracing the web of his relationships with the various departments of his business. Amory Blaine and Antony Patch were romantic projections of the author; Gatsby and Dick Diver were conceived more or less objectively, but not very profoundly explored. Monroe Stahr is really created from within at the same time that he is criticized by an intelligence that has now become sure of itself and knows how to assign him to his proper place in a larger scheme of things.

The Last Tycoon is thus, even in its imperfect state, Fitzgerald's most mature piece of work. It is marked off also from his other novels by the fact that it is the first to deal seriously with any profession or business. The earlier books of Fitzgerald had been preoccupied with debutantes and college boys, with the fast lives of the wild spenders of the twenties. The main activities of the people in these stories, the occasions for which they live, are big parties at which they go off like fireworks and which are likely to leave them in pieces. But the parties in *The Last Tycoon* are incidental and unimportant; Monroe Stahr, unlike any other of Scott Fitzgerald's heroes, is inextricably involved with an industry of which he has been one of the creators, and its fate will be implied by his tragedy. The moving-picture business in America has here been observed at a close range, studied with a careful attention and dramatized with a sharp wit such as are not to be found in combination in any of the other novels on the subject. *The Last Tycoon* is far and away the best novel we have had about Hollywood, and it is the only one which takes us inside.

It has been possible to supplement this unfinished draft with an outline of the rest of the story as Fitzgerald intended to develop it, and with passages from the author's notes which deal, often vividly, with the characters and scenes.

EDMUND WILSON
1941

THE LAST TYCOON

THE LAST TYCOON

CHAPTER I

THOUGH I HAVEN'T ever been on the screen I was brought up in pictures. Rudolph Valentino came to my fifth birthday party— or so I was told. I put this down only to indicate that even before the age of reason I was in a position to watch the wheels go round.

I was going to write my memoirs once, *The Producer's Daughter,* but at eighteen you never quite get around to anything like that. It's just as well—it would have been as flat as an old column of Lolly Parsons'. My father was in the picture business as another man might be in cotton or steel, and I took it tranquilly. At the worst I accepted Hollywood with the resignation of a ghost assigned to a haunted house. I knew what you were supposed to think about it but I was obstinately unhorrified.

This is easy to say, but harder to make people understand. When I was at Bennington some of the English teachers who pretended an indifference to Hollywood or its products, really *hated* it. Hated it way down deep as a threat to their existence. Even before that, when I was in a convent, a sweet little nun asked me to get her a script of a screen play so she could "teach her class about movie writing" as she had taught them about the essay and the short story. I got the script for her, and I suppose she puzzled over it and puzzled over it, but it was never mentioned in class, and she gave it back to me with an air of offended surprise and not a single comment. That's what I half expect to happen to this story.

You can take Hollywood for granted like I did, or you can dismiss it with the contempt we reserve for what we don't understand. It can be understood too, but only dimly and in flashes. Not half a dozen men have ever been able to keep the whole equation of pictures in their heads. And perhaps the closest a woman can come to the set-up is to try and understand one of those men.

The world from an airplane I knew. Father always had us travel back and forth that way from school and college. After my sister died when I was a junior, I travelled to and fro alone, and the journey always made me think of her, made me somewhat solemn and subdued. Sometimes there were picture people I knew on board the plane, and occasionally there was an attractive college boy—but not often during the depression. I seldom really fell asleep during the trip, what with thoughts of Eleanor and the sense of that sharp rip between coast and coast—at least not till we had left those lonely little airports in Tennessee.

This trip was so rough that the passengers divided early into those who turned in right away and those who didn't want to turn in at all. There were two of these latter right across from me, and I was pretty sure from their fragmentary conversation that they were from Hollywood—one of them because he looked like it: a middle-aged Jew, who alternately talked with nervous excitement or else crouched as if ready to spring, in a harrowing silence; the other a pale, plain, stocky man of thirty, whom I was sure I had seen before. He had been to the house or something. But it might have been when I was a little girl, and so I wasn't offended that he didn't recognize me.

The stewardess—she was tall, handsome and flashing dark, a type that they seemed to run to—asked me if she could make up my berth.

"—and, dear, do you want an aspirin?" She perched on the side of the seat and rocked precariously to and fro with the June hurricane, "—or nembutal?"

"No."

"I've been so busy with everyone else that I've had no time to ask you." She sat down beside me and buckled us both in. "Do you want some gum?"

This reminded me to get rid of the piece that had been boring me for hours. I wrapped it in a piece of magazine and put it into the automatic ash-holder.

"I can always tell people are nice," the stewardess said approvingly, "if they wrap their gum in paper before they put it in there."

We sat for awhile in the half-light of the swaying car. It was vaguely like a swanky restaurant at that twilight time between meals. We were all lingering—and not quite on purpose. Even the stewardess, I think, had to keep reminding herself why she was there.

She and I talked about a young actress I knew, whom she had flown West with two years before. It was in the very lowest time of the depression, and the young actress kept staring out the window in such an intent way that the stewardess was afraid she was contemplating a leap. It appeared though that she was not afraid of poverty, but only of revolution.

"I know what mother and *I* are going to do," she confided to the stewardess. "We're coming out to the Yellowstone and we're just going to live simply till it all blows over. Then we'll come back. They don't kill artists—you know?"

The proposition pleased me. It conjured up a pretty picture of the actress and her mother being fed by kind Tory bears who brought them honey, and by gentle fawns who fetched extra milk from the does and then lingered near to make pillows for their heads at night. In turn I told the stewardess about the lawyer and the director who told their plans to Father one night in those brave days. If the bonus army conquered Washington, the lawyer had a boat hidden in the Sacramento River, and he was going to row up stream for a few months and then come back "because they always needed lawyers after a revolution to straighten out the legal side."

The director had tended more toward defeatism. He had an old suit, shirt and shoes in waiting—he never did say whether they were his own or whether he got them from the prop department—and he was going to Disappear into the Crowd. I remember Father saying: "But they'll look at your hands! They'll know you haven't done manual work for years. And they'll ask for your union card." And I remember how the director's face fell, and how gloomy he was while he ate his dessert, and how funny and puny they sounded to me.

"Is your father an actor, Miss Brady?" asked the stewardess. "I've certainly heard the name."

At the name Brady, both the men across the aisle looked up. Sidewise—that Hollywood look, that always seems thrown over one shoulder. Then the young, pale, stocky man unbuttoned his safety strap and stood in the aisle beside us.

"Are you Cecilia *Brady*?" he demanded accusingly, as if I'd been holding out on him. "I *thought* I recognized you. I'm Wylie White."

He could have omitted this—for at the same moment a new voice said, "Watch your step, Wylie!", and another man brushed by him in the aisle and went forward in the direction of the cockpit. Wylie White started, and a little too late called after him defiantly: "I only take orders from the pilot."

I recognized the kind of pleasantry that goes on between the powers in Hollywood and their satellites.

The stewardess reproved him:

"Not so loud, please—some of the passengers are asleep."

I saw now that the other man across the aisle, the middle-aged Jew, was on his feet also, staring, with shameless economic lechery, after the man who had just gone by. Or rather at the back of the man, who gestured sideways with his hand in a sort of farewell, as he went out of my sight.

I asked the stewardess: "Is he the as*sis*tant pilot?"

She was unbuckling our belt, about to abandon me to Wylie White.

"No. That's Mr. Smith. He has the private compartment, the 'bridal suite'—only he has it alone. The assistant pilot is always in uniform." She stood up: "I want to find out if we're going to be grounded in Nashville."

Wylie White was aghast.

"Why?"

"It's a storm coming up the Mississippi Valley."

"Does that mean we'll have to stay here all *night?*"

"If this keeps up!"

A sudden dip indicated that it would. It tipped Wylie White into the seat opposite me, shunted the stewardess precipitately down in the direction of the cockpit, and plunked the Jewish man into a sitting position. After the studied, unruffled exclamations of distaste that befitted the air-minded, we settled down. There was an introduction.

"Miss Brady—Mr. Schwartz," said Wylie White. "He's a great friend of your father's, too."

Mr. Schwartz nodded so vehemently that I could almost hear him saying: "It's true. As God is my judge, it's true!"

He might have said this right out loud at one time in his life—but he was obviously a man to whom something had happened. Meeting him was like encountering a friend who has been in a fist fight or collision, and got flattened. You stare at your friend and say: "What happened to you?" And he answers something unintelligible through broken teeth and swollen lips. He can't even tell you about it.

Mr. Schwartz was physically unmarked; the exaggerated Persian nose and oblique eye-shadow were as congenital as the tip-tilted Irish redness around my father's nostrils.

"Nashville!" cried Wylie White. "That means we go to a hotel. We don't get to the coast till tomorrow night—if then. My God! I was born in Nashville."

"I should think you'd like to see it again."

"Never—I've kept away for fifteen years. I hope I'll *never* see it again."

But he would—for the plane was unmistakably going down, down, down, like Alice in the rabbit hole. Cupping my hand against the window I saw the blur of the city far away on the left. The green sign "Fasten your belts—No smoking" had been on since we first rode into the storm.

"Did you hear what he said?" said Schwartz from one of his fiery silences across the aisle.

"Hear what?" asked Wylie.

"Hear what he's calling himself," said Schwartz. "Mr. *Smith*!"

"Why not?" asked Wylie.

"Oh nothing," said Schwartz quickly. "I just thought it was funny, Smith." I never heard a laugh with less mirth in it: "Smith!"

I suppose there has been nothing like the airports since the days of the stage-stops—nothing quite as lonely, as somber-silent. The old red-brick depots were built right into the towns they marked—people didn't get off at those isolated stations unless they lived there. But airports lead you way back in history like oases, like the stops on the great trade routes. The sight of air travellers strolling in ones and twos into midnight airports will draw a small crowd any night up to two. The young people look at the planes, the older ones look at the passengers with a watchful incredulity. In the big transcontinental planes we were the coastal rich, who casually alighted from our cloud in mid-America. High adventure might be among us, disguised as a movie star. But mostly it wasn't. And I always wished fervently that we looked more interesting than we did—just as I often have at premières, when the fans look at you with scornful reproach because you're not a star.

On the ground Wylie and I were suddenly friends, because he held out his arm to steady me when I got out of the plane. From then on, he made a dead set for me—and I didn't mind. From the moment we walked into the airport it had become plain that if we were stranded here we were stranded here together. (It wasn't like the time I lost my boy—the time my boy played the piano with that girl Reina in a little New England farmhouse near Bennington, and I realized at last I wasn't wanted. Guy Lombardo was on the air playing *Top Hat* and *Cheek to Cheek,* and she taught him the melodies. The keys falling like leaves and her hands splayed over his as she showed him a black chord. I was a freshman then.)

When we went into the airport Mr. Schwartz was along with us, too, but he seemed in a sort of dream. All the time we were trying to get accurate information at the desk, he kept staring at the door that led out to the landing field, as if he were afraid the plane would leave without him. Then I excused myself for a few minutes and something happened that I didn't see, but when I came back he and White were standing close together, White talking and Schwartz looking twice as much as if a great truck had just backed up over him. He didn't stare at the door to the landing field any more. I heard the end of Wylie White's remark . . .

"—I told you to shut up. It serves you right."

"I only said——"

He broke off as I came up and asked if there was any news. It was then half-past two in the morning.

"A little," said Wylie White. "They don't think we'll be able to start for three hours anyhow, so some of the softies are going to a hotel. But I'd like to take you out to the Hermitage, Home of Andrew Jackson."

"How could we see it in the dark?" demanded Schwartz.

"Hell, it'll be sunrise in two hours."

"You two go," said Schwartz.

"All right—you take the bus to the hotel. It's still waiting—*he's* in there." Wylie's voice had a taunt in it. "Maybe it'd be a good thing."

"No, I'll go along with you," said Schwartz hastily.

We took a taxi in the sudden country dark outside, and he seemed to cheer up. He patted my knee-cap encouragingly.

"I should go along," he said, "I should be chaperone. Once upon a time when I was in the big money, I had a daughter—a beautiful daughter."

He spoke as if she had been sold to creditors as a tangible asset.

"You'll have another," Wylie assured him. "You'll get it all back. Another turn of the wheel and you'll be where Cecilia's papa is, won't he, Cecilia?"

"Where is this Hermitage?" asked Schwartz presently. "Far away at the end of nowhere? Will we miss the plane?"

"Skip it," said Wylie. "We ought to've brought the stewardess along for you. Didn't you admire the stewardess? *I* thought she was pretty cute."

We drove for a long time over a bright level countryside, just a road and a tree and a shack and a tree, and then suddenly along a winding twist of woodland. I could feel even in the darkness that the trees of the woodland were green—that it was all different from the dusty olive-tint of California. Somewhere we passed a negro driving three cows ahead of him, and they mooed as he scatted them to the side of the road. They were real cows, with warm, fresh, silky flanks, and the negro grew gradually real out of the darkness with his big brown eyes staring at us close to the car, as Wylie gave him a quarter. He said "*Thank* you—thank you," and stood there, and the cows mooed again into the night as we drove off.

I thought of the first sheep I ever remember seeing—hundreds of them, and how our car drove suddenly into them on the back lot of the old Laemmle studio. They were unhappy about being in pictures, but the men in the car with us kept saying:

"Swell?"

"Is that what you wanted, Dick?"

"Isn't that swell?" And the man named Dick kept standing up in the car as if he were Cortez or Balboa, looking over that gray fleecy undulation. If I ever knew what picture they were in, I have long forgotten.

We had driven an hour. We crossed a brook over an old rattly iron bridge laid with planks. Now there were roosters crowing and blue-green shadows stirring every time we passed a farmhouse.

"I told you it'd be morning soon," said Wylie. "I was born near here—the son of impoverished southern paupers. The family mansion is now used as an outhouse. We had four servants—my father, my mother and my two sisters. I refused to join the guild, and so I went to Memphis to start my career, which has now reached a dead end." He put his arm around me: "Cecilia, will you marry me, so I can share the Brady fortune?"

He was disarming enough, so I let my head lie on his shoulder. "What do you do, Celia. Go to school?"

"I go to Bennington. I'm a junior."

"Oh, I beg your pardon. I should have known, but I never had the advantage of college training. But a *ju*nior—why I read in *Esquire* that juniors have nothing to learn, Cecilia."

"Why do people think that college girls——"

"Don't apologize—knowledge is power."

"You'd know from the way you talk that we were on our way to Hollywood," I said. "It's always years and years behind the times."

He pretended to be shocked.

"You mean girls in the East have no private lives?"

"That's the point. They *have* got private lives. You're bothering me, let go."

"I can't. It might wake Schwartz, and I think this is the first sleep he's had for weeks. Listen, Cecilia: I once had an affair with the wife of a producer. A very short affair. When it was over she said to me in no uncertain terms, she said: 'Don't you ever tell about this or I'll have you thrown out of Hollywood. My husband's a much more important man than you!' "

I liked him again now, and presently the taxi turned down a long lane fragrant with honeysuckle and narcissus, and stopped beside the great grey hulk of the Andrew Jackson house. The driver turned around to tell us something about it, but Wylie shushed him, pointing at Schwartz, and we tiptoed out of the car.

"You can't get into the Mansion now," the taxi man told us politely.

Wylie and I went and sat against the wide pillars of the steps.

"What about Mr. Schwartz," I asked. "Who is he?"

"To hell with Schwartz. He was the head of some combine once —First National? Paramount? United Artists? Now he's down and out. But he'll be back. You can't flunk out of pictures unless you're a dope or a drunk."

"You don't like Hollywood," I suggested.

"Yes I do. Sure I do. Say! This isn't anything to talk about on the steps of Andrew Jackson's house—at dawn."

"I *like* Hollywood," I persisted.

"It's all right. It's a mining town in lotus land. Who said that? I did. It's a good place for toughies, but I went there from Savannah, Georgia. I went to a garden party the first day. My host shook hands and left me. It was all there—that swimming pool, green moss at two dollars an inch, beautiful felines having drinks and fun——

"—And nobody spoke to me. Not a soul. I spoke to half a dozen people but they didn't answer. That continued for an hour, two hours—then I got up from where I was sitting and ran out at a dog trot like a crazy man. I didn't feel I had any rightful identity until I got back to the hotel and the clerk handed me a letter addressed to me in my name."

Naturally I hadn't ever had such an experience, but looking back on parties I'd been to, I realized that such things could happen. We don't go for strangers in Hollywood unless they wear a sign saying that their axe has been thoroughly ground elsewhere, and that in any case it's not going to fall on our necks—in other words, unless they're a celebrity. And they'd better look out even then.

"You should have risen above it," I said smugly. "It's not a slam at *you* when people are rude—it's a slam at the people they've met before."

"Such a pretty girl—to say such wise things."

There was an eager to-do in the eastern sky, and Wylie could see me plain—thin with good features and lots of style, and the kicking fetus of a mind. I wonder what I looked like in that dawn, five years ago. A little rumpled and pale, I suppose, but at that age, when one has the young illusion that most adventures are good, I needed only a bath and a change to go on for hours.

Wylie stared at me with really flattering appreciation—and then suddenly we were not alone. Mr. Schwartz wandered apologetically into the pretty scene.

"I fell upon a large metal handle," he said, touching the corner of his eye.

Wylie jumped up.

"Just in time, Mr. Schwartz," he said. "The tour is just starting. Home of Old Hickory—America's tenth president. The victor of New Orleans, opponent of the National Bank, and inventor of the Spoils System."

Schwartz looked toward me as toward a jury.

"There's a writer for you," he said. "Knows everything and at the same time he knows nothing."

"What's that?" said Wylie, indignant.

It was my first inkling that he was a writer. And while I like writers—because if you ask a writer anything, you usually get an answer—still it belittled him in my eyes. Writers aren't people exactly. Or, if they're any good, they're a whole *lot* of people trying so hard to be one person. It's like actors, who try so pathetically not to look in mirrors. Who lean *back*ward trying—only to see their faces in the reflecting chandeliers.

"Ain't writers like that, Celia?" demanded Schwartz. "I have no words for them. I only know it's true."

Wylie looked at him with slowly gathering indignation. "I've heard that before," he said. "Look, Manny, I'm a more practical man than you any day! I've sat in an office and listened to some mystic stalk up and down for hours spouting tripe that'd land him on a nut-farm anywhere outside of California—and then at the end tell me how *prac*tical he was, and *I* was a dreamer—and would I kindly go away and make sense out of what he'd said."

Mr. Schwartz's face fell into its more disintegrated alignments. One eye looked upward through the tall elms. He raised his hand and bit without interest at the cuticle on his second finger. There was a bird flying about the chimney of the house, and his glance followed it. It perched on the chimney pot like a raven, and Mr. Schwartz's eyes remained fixed upon it as he said: "We can't get in, and it's time for you two to go back to the plane."

It was still not quite dawn. The Hermitage looked like a nice big white box, but a little lonely and vacated still after a hundred years. We walked back to the car. Only after we had gotten in, and Mr. Schwartz had surprisingly shut the taxi door on us, did we realize he didn't intend to come along.

"I'm not going to the Coast—I decided that when I woke up. So I'll stay here, and afterwards the driver could come back for me."

"Going back East?" said Wylie with surprise. "Just because——"

"I have decided," said Schwartz, faintly smiling. "Once I used to be a regular man of decision—you'd be surprised." He felt in his pocket, as the taxi driver warmed up the engine. "Will you give this note to Mr. Smith?"

"Shall I come in two hours?" the driver asked Schwartz.

"Yes . . . sure. I shall be glad to entertain myself looking around."

I kept thinking of him all the way back to the airport—trying to fit him into that early hour and into that landscape. He had come a long way from some ghetto to present himself at that raw shrine. Manny Schwartz and Andrew Jackson—it was hard to say them in the same sentence. It was doubtful if he knew who Andrew Jackson was as he wandered around, but perhaps he figured that if people had preserved his house Andrew Jackson must have been someone who was large and merciful, able to understand. At both ends of life man needed nourishment: a breast—a shrine. Something to lay himself beside when no one wanted him further, and shoot a bullet into his head.

Of course we did not know this for twenty hours. When we got to the airport we told the purser that Mr. Schwartz was not continuing, and then forgot about him. The storm had wandered away into Eastern Tennessee and broken against the mountains, and we were taking off in less than an hour. Sleepy-eyed travellers appeared from the hotel, and I dozed a few minutes on one of those Iron Maidens they use for couches. Slowly the idea of a perilous journey was recreated out of the debris of our failure: a new stewardess, tall, handsome, flashing dark, exactly like the other except she wore seersucker instead of Frenchy red-and-blue, went briskly past us with a suitcase. Wylie sat beside me as we waited.

"Did you give the note to Mr. Smith?" I asked, half asleep.

"Yeah."

"Who is Mr. Smith? I suspect he spoiled Mr. Schwartz's trip."

"It was Schwartz's fault."

"I'm prejudiced against steam-rollers," I said. "My father tries to be a steam-roller around the house, and I tell him to save it for the studio."

I wondered if I was being fair; words are the palest counters at that time in the morning. "Still, he steam-rollered me into Bennington and I've always been grateful for that."

"There would be quite a crash," Wylie said, "if steam-roller Brady met steam-roller Smith."

"Is Mr. Smith a competitor of Father's?"

"Not exactly. I should say no. But if he was a competitor, I know where my money would be."

"On Father?"

"I'm afraid not."

It was too early in the morning for family patriotism. The pilot was at the desk with the purser and he shook his head as they regarded a prospective passenger who had put two nickels in the electric phonograph and lay alcoholically on a bench fighting off sleep. The first song he had chosen, "Lost," thundered through the room, followed, after a slight interval, by his other choice, "Gone," which was equally dogmatic and final. The pilot shook his head emphatically and walked over to the passenger.

"Afraid we're not going to be able to carry you this time, old man."

"Wha?"

The drunk sat up, awful-looking, yet discernibly attractive, and I was sorry for him in spite of his passionately ill-chosen music.

"Go back to the hotel and get some sleep. There'll be another plane tonight."

"Only going up in ee *air*."

"Not this time, old man."

In his disappointment the drunk fell off the bench—and above the phonograph, a loudspeaker summoned us respectable people outside. In the corridor of the plane I ran into Monroe Stahr and fell all over him, or wanted to. There was a man any girl would go for, with or without encouragement. I was emphatically with*out* it, but he liked me and sat down opposite till the plane took off.

"Let's all ask for our money back," he suggested. His dark eyes took me in, and I wondered what they would look like if he fell in love. They were kind, aloof and, though they often reasoned with you gently, somewhat superior. It was no fault of theirs if they saw so much. He darted in and out of the role of "one of the boys" with dexterity—but on the whole I should say he wasn't one of them. But he knew how to shut up, how to draw into the background, how to listen. From where he stood (and though he was not a tall man, it always seemed high up) he watched the multitudinous practicalities of his world like a proud young shepherd to whom night and day had never mattered. He was born sleepless, without a talent for rest or the desire for it.

We sat in unembarrassed silence—I had known him since he became Father's partner a dozen years ago, when I was seven and Stahr was twenty-two. Wylie was across the aisle and I didn't know whether or not to introduce them, but Stahr kept turning his ring so abstractedly that he made me feel young and invisible, and I didn't dare. I never dared look quite away from him or quite *at* him, unless I had something important to say—and I knew he affected many other people in the same manner.

"I'll *give* you this ring, Cecilia."

"I beg your pardon. I didn't realize that I was——"

"I've got half a dozen like it."

He handed it to me, a gold nugget with the letter S in bold relief. I had been thinking how oddly its bulk contrasted with his fingers, which were delicate and slender like the rest of his body, and like his slender face with the arched eyebrows and the dark curly hair. He looked spiritual at times, but he was a fighter—somebody out of his past knew him when he was one of a gang of kids in the Bronx, and gave me a description of how he walked always at the head of his gang, this rather frail boy, occasionally throwing a command backward out of the corner of his mouth.

Stahr folded my hand over the ring, stood up and addressed Wylie.

"Come up to the bridal suite," he said. "See you later, Cecilia."

Before they went out of hearing, I heard Wylie's question: "Did you open Schwartz's note?" And Stahr:

"Not yet."

I must be slow, for only then did I realize that Stahr was Mr. Smith.

Afterwards Wylie told me what was in the note. Written by the headlights of the taxi, it was almost illegible.

"Dear Monroe, You are the best of them all I have always admired your mentality so when you turn against me I know it's no use! I must be no good and am not going to continue the journey let me warn you once again look out! I know.

"Your friend

MANNY."

Stahr read it twice, and raised his hand to the morning stubble on his chin.

"He's a nervous wreck," he said. "There's nothing to be done—absolutely nothing. I'm sorry I was short with him—but I don't like a man to approach me telling me it's for *my* sake."

"Maybe it was," said Wylie.

"It's poor technique."

"I'd fall for it," said Wylie. "I'm vain as a woman. If anybody pretends to be interested in me, I'll ask for more. I like advice."

Stahr shook his head distastefully. Wylie kept on ribbing him—he was one of those to whom this privilege was permitted.

"You fall for some kinds of flattery," he said. "This 'little Napoleon stuff.'"

"It makes me sick," said Stahr, "but it's not as bad as some man trying to help you."

"If you don't like advice, why do you pay *me*?"

"That's a question of merchandise," said Stahr. "I'm a merchant. I want to buy what's in your mind."

"You're no merchant," said Wylie. "I knew a lot of them when I was a publicity man, and I agree with Charles Francis Adams."

"What did he say?"

"He knew them all—Gould, Vanderbilt, Carnegie, Astor—and he said there wasn't one he'd care to meet again in the hereafter. Well —they haven't improved since then, and that's why I say you're no merchant."

"Adams was probably a sourbelly," said Stahr. "He wanted to be head man himself, but he didn't have the judgment or else the character."

"He had brains," said Wylie rather tartly.

"It takes more than brains. You writers and artists poop out and get all mixed up, and somebody has to come in and straighten you out." He shrugged his shoulders. "You seem to take things so personally, hating people and worshipping them—always thinking people are so important—especially yourselves. You just ask to be kicked around. I like people and I like them to like me, but I wear my heart where God put it—on the inside."

He broke off.

"What did I say to Schwartz in the airport? Do you remember —exactly?"

"You said, 'Whatever you're after, the answer is No!' "

Stahr was silent.

"He was sunk," said Wylie, "but I laughed him out of it. We took Billy Brady's daughter for a ride."

Stahr rang for the stewardess.

"That pilot," he said, "would he mind if I sat up in front with him awhile?"

"That's against the rules, Mr. Smith."

"Ask him to step in here a minute when he's free."

Stahr sat up front all afternoon. While we slid off the endless desert and over the table-lands, dyed with many colors like the white sands we dyed with colors when I was a child. Then in the late afternoon, the peaks themselves—the Mountains of the Frozen Saw —slid under our propellers and we were close to home.

When I wasn't dozing I was thinking that I wanted to marry Stahr, that I wanted to make him love me. Oh, the conceit! What on earth did I have to offer? But I didn't think like that then. I had the pride of young women, which draws its strength from such sublime thoughts as "I'm as good as *she* is." For my purposes I was just as beautiful as the great beauties who must have inevitably thrown themselves at his head. My little spurt of intellectual interest was of course making me fit to be a brilliant ornament of any salon.

I know now it was absurd. Though Stahr's education was founded on nothing more than a night-school course in stenography, he had a long time ago run ahead through trackless wastes of perception into fields where very few men were able to follow him. But in my reckless conceit I matched my grey eyes against his brown ones for guile, my young golf-and-tennis heart-beats against his, which must be slowing a little after years of over-work. And I planned and I contrived and I plotted—any woman can tell you—but it never came to anything, as you will see. I still like to think that if he'd been a poor boy and nearer my age I could have managed it, but of course the real truth was that I had nothing to offer that he didn't have; some of my more romantic ideas actually stemmed from pictures— *42nd Street*, for example, had a great influence on me. It's more than possible that some of the pictures which Stahr himself conceived had shaped me into what I was.

So it was rather hopeless. Emotionally, at least, people can't live by taking in each other's washing.

But at that time it was different: Father might help, the stewardess might help. She might go up in the cockpit and say to Stahr: "If I ever saw love, it's in that girl's eyes."

The pilot might help: "Man, are you blind? Why don't you go back there?"

Wylie White might help—instead of standing in the aisle looking at me doubtfully, wondering whether I was awake or asleep.

"Sit down," I said. "What's new?—where are we?"

"Up in the air."

"Oh, so that's it. Sit down." I tried to show a cheerful interest: "What are you writing?"

"Heaven help me, I am writing about a Boy Scout—*The* Boy Scout."

"Is it Stahr's idea?"

"I don't know—he told me to look into it. He may have ten writers working ahead of me or behind me, a system which he so thoughtfully invented. So you're in love with him?"

"I should say not," I said indignantly. "I've known him all my life."

"Desperate, eh? Well, I'll arrange it if you'll use all your influence to advance me. I want a unit of my own."

I closed my eyes again and drifted off. When I woke up, the stewardess was putting a blanket over me.

"Almost there," she said.

Out the window I could see by the sunset that we were in a greener land.

"I just heard something funny," she volunteered, "up in the cockpit—that Mr. Smith—or Mr. Stahr—I never remember seeing his name—"

"It's never on any pictures," I said.

"Oh. Well, he's been asking the pilots a lot about flying—I mean he's interested? You *know*?"

"I know."

"I mean one of them told me he bet he could teach Mr. Stahr solo flying in ten minutes. He has such a fine mentality, that's what he said."

I was getting impatient.

"Well, what was so funny?"

"Well, finally one of the pilots asked Mr. Smith if he liked his business, and Mr. Smith said, 'Sure. Sure I like it. It's nice being the only sound nut in a hatful of cracked ones.'"

The stewardess doubled up with laughter—and I could have spit at her.

"I mean calling all those people a hatful of nuts. I mean *cracked* nuts." Her laughter stopped with unexpected suddenness, and her face was grave as she stood up. "Well, I've got to finish my chart."

"Goodbye."

Obviously Stahr had put the pilots right up on the throne with him and let them rule with him for awhile. Years later I travelled with one of those same pilots and he told me one thing Stahr had said.

He was looking down at the mountains.

"Suppose you were a railroad man," he said. "You have to send a train through there somewhere. Well, you get your surveyors' reports, and you find there's three or four or half a dozen gaps, and not one is better than the other. You've got to decide—on what basis? You can't test the best way—except by doing it. So you just do it."

The pilot thought he had missed something.

"How do you mean?"

"You choose some one way for no reason at all—because that mountain's pink or the blueprint is a better blue. You see?"

The pilot considered that this was very valuable advice. But he doubted if he'd ever be in a position to apply it.

"What I wanted to know," he told me ruefully, "is how he ever got to be Mr. Stahr."

I'm afraid Stahr could never have answered that one; for the embryo is not equipped with a memory. But I could answer a little. He had flown up very high to see, on strong wings, when he was young. And while he was up there he had looked on all the kingdoms, with the kind of eyes that can stare straight into the sun. Beating his wings tenaciously—finally frantically—and keeping on beating them, he had stayed up there longer than most of us, and then, remembering all he had seen from his great height of how things were, he had settled gradually to earth.

The motors were off, and all our five senses began to readjust themselves for landing. I could see a line of lights for the Long Beach Naval Station ahead and to the left, and on the right a twinkling blur for Santa Monica. The California moon was out, huge and orange over the Pacific. However I happened to feel about these things—and they were home, after all—I know that Stahr must have felt much more. These were the things I had first opened my eyes on, like the sheep on the back lot of the old Laemmle studio; but this was where Stahr had come to earth after that extraordinary illuminating flight where he saw which way we were going, and how we looked doing it, and how much of it mattered. You could say that this was where an accidental wind blew him, but I don't think so. I would rather think that in a "long shot" he saw a new way of measuring our jerky hopes and graceful rogueries and awkward sorrows, and that he came here from choice to be with us to the end. Like the plane coming down into the Glendale airport, into the warm darkness.

CHAPTER II

It was nine o'clock of a July night and there were still some extras in the drug-store across from the studio—I could see them bent over the pin-games inside—as I parked my car. "Old" Johnny Swanson stood on the corner in his semi-cowboy clothes, staring gloomily past the moon. Once he had been as big in pictures as Tom Mix or Bill Hart—now it was too sad to speak to him, and I hurried across the street and through the front gate.

There is never a time when a studio is absolutely quiet. There is always a night shift of technicians in the laboratories and dubbing rooms and people on the maintenance staff dropping in at the commissary. But the sounds are all different—the padded hush of tires, the quiet tick of a motor running idle, the naked cry of a soprano singing into a nightbound microphone. Around a corner I came upon a man in rubber boots washing down a car in a wonderful white light—a fountain among the dead industrial shadows. I slowed up as I saw Mr. Marcus being hoisted into his car in front of the administration building, because he took so long to say anything, even good night—and while I waited I realized that the soprano was singing, *Come, come, I love you only* over and over; I remember this because she kept singing the same line during the earthquake. That didn't come for five minutes yet.

Father's offices were in the old building with the long balconies and iron rails with their suggestion of a perpetual tightrope. Father was on the second floor, with Stahr on one side and Mr. Marcus on the other—this evening there were lights all along the row. My stomach dipped a little at the proximity to Stahr, but that was in pretty good control now—I'd seen him only once in the month I'd been home.

There were a lot of strange things about Father's office, but I'll make it brief. In the outer part were three poker-faced secretaries who

21

had sat there like witches ever since I could remember—Birdy Peters, Maude something, and Rosemary Schmiel; I don't know whether this was her name, but she was the dean of the trio, so to speak, and under her desk was the kick-lock that admitted you to Father's throne room. All three of the secretaries were passionate capitalists, and Birdy had invented the rule that if typists were seen eating together more than once in a single week, they were hauled up on the carpet. At that time the studios feared mob rule.

I went on in. Nowadays all chief executives have huge drawing rooms, but my father's was the first. It was also the first to have one-way glass in the big French windows, and I've heard a story about a trap in the floor that would drop unpleasant visitors to an oubliette below, but believe it to be an invention. There was a big painting of Will Rogers, hung conspicuously and intended, I think, to suggest Father's essential kinship with Hollywood's St. Francis; there was a signed photograph of Minna Davis, Stahr's dead wife, and photos of other studio celebrities and big chalk drawings of mother and me. Tonight the one-way French windows were open and a big moon, rosy-gold with a haze around, was wedged helpless in one of them. Father and Jacques La Borwitz and Rosemary Schmiel were down at the end around a big circular desk.

What did Father look like? I couldn't describe him except for once in New York when I met him where I didn't expect to; I was aware of a bulky, middle-aged man who looked a little ashamed of himself, and I wished he'd move on—and then I saw he was Father. Afterward I was shocked at my impression. Father can be very magnetic—he has a tough jaw and an Irish smile.

But as for Jacques La Borwitz, I shall spare you. Let me just say he was an assistant producer, which is something like a commissar, and let it go at that. Where Stahr picked up such mental cadavers or had them forced upon him—or especially how he got any use out of them—has always amazed me, as it amazed everyone fresh from the East who slapped up against them. Jacques La Borwitz had his points, no doubt, but so have the sub-microscopic protozoa, so has a dog prowling for a bitch and a bone. Jacques La—oh my!

From their expressions I was sure they had been talking about Stahr. Stahr had ordered something or forbidden something, or defied Father or junked one of La Borwitz' pictures or something catastrophic, and they were sitting there in protest at night in a community of rebellion and helplessness. Rosemary Schmiel sat pad in hand, as if ready to write down their dejection.

"I'm to drive you home dead or alive," I told Father. "All those birthday presents rotting away in their packages!"

"A birthday!" cried Jacques in a flurry of apology. "How old? I didn't know."

"Forty-three," said Father distinctly.

He was older than that—four years—and Jacques knew it; I saw him note it down in his account book to use some time. Out here these account books are carried open in the hand. One can see the entries being made without recourse to lip-reading, and Rosemary Schmiel was compelled in emulation to make a mark on her pad. As she rubbed it out, the earth quaked under us.

We didn't get the full shock like at Long Beach, where the upper stories of shops were spewed into the streets and small hotels drifted out to sea—but for a full minute our bowels were one with the bowels of the earth—like some nightmare attempt to attach our navel cords again and jerk us back to the womb of creation.

Mother's picture fell off the wall, revealing a small safe—Rosemary and I grabbed frantically for each other and did a strange screaming waltz across the room. Jacques fainted or at least disappeared, and Father clung to his desk and shouted, "Are you all right?" Outside the window the singer came to the climax of *I love you only,* held it a moment and then, I swear, started it all over. Or maybe they were playing it back to her from the recording machine.

The room stood still, shimmying a little. We made our way to the door, suddenly including Jacques, who had reappeared, and tottered out dizzily through the anteroom on to the iron balcony. Almost all the lights were out, and from here and there we could hear cries and calls. Momentarily we stood waiting for a second shock—then, as with a common impulse, we went into Stahr's entry and through to his office.

The office was big, but not as big as Father's. Stahr sat on the side of his couch rubbing his eyes. When the quake came he had been asleep, and he wasn't sure yet whether he had dreamed it. When we convinced him he thought it was all rather funny—until the telephones began to ring. I watched him as unobtrusively as possible.

He was grey with fatigue while he listened to the phone and dictograph; but as the reports came in, his eyes began to pick up shine.

"A couple of water mains have burst," he said to Father, "—they're heading into the back lot."

"Gray's shooting in the French Village," said Father.

"It's flooded around the Station, too, and in the Jungle and the City Corner. What the hell—nobody seems to be hurt." In passing, he shook my hands gravely: "Where've you been, Cecilia?"

"You going out there, Monroe?" Father asked.

"When all the news is in. One of the power lines is off, too—I've sent for Robinson."

He made me sit down with him on the couch and tell about the quake again.

"You look tired," I said, cute and motherly.

"Yes," he agreed, "I've got no place to go in the evenings, so I just work."

"I'll arrange some evenings for you."

"I used to play poker with a gang," he said thoughtfully, "before I was married. But they all drank themselves to death."

Miss Doolan, his secretary, came in with fresh bad news.

"Robby'll take care of everything when he comes," Stahr assured Father. He turned to me. "Now there's a man—that Robinson. He was a trouble-shooter—fixed the telephone wires in Minnesota blizzards—nothing stumps him. He'll be here in a minute—you'll like Robby."

He said it as if it had been his life-long intention to bring us together, and he had arranged the whole earthquake with just that in mind.

"Yes, you'll like Robby," he repeated. "When do you go back to college?"

"I've just come home."

"You get the whole summer?"

"I'm sorry," I said. "I'll go back as soon as I can."

I was in a mist. It hadn't failed to cross my mind that he might have some intention about me, but if it was so, it was in an exasperatingly early stage—I was merely "a good property." And the idea didn't seem so attractive at that moment—like marrying a doctor. He seldom left the studio before eleven.

"How long," he asked my father, "before she graduates from college. That's what I was trying to say."

And I think I was about to sing out eagerly that I needn't go back at all, that I was quite educated already—when the totally admirable Robinson came in. He was a bowlegged young redhead, all ready to go.

"This is Robby, Cecilia," said Stahr. "Come on, Robby."

So I met Robby. I can't say it seemed like fate—but it was. For it was Robby who later told me how Stahr found his love that night.

Under the moon the back lot was thirty acres of fairyland—not because the locations really looked like African jungles and French châteaux and schooners at anchor and Broadway by night, but because they looked like the torn picture books of childhood, like fragments of stories dancing in an open fire. I never lived in a house with an attic, but a back lot must be something like that, and at night of course in an enchanted distorted way, it all comes true.

When Stahr and Robby arrived, clusters of lights had already picked out the danger spots in the flood.

"We'll pump it out into the swamp on Thirty-Sixth Street," said Robby after a moment. "It's city property—but isn't this an act of God? Say—look there!"

On top of a huge head of the Goddess Siva, two women were floating down the current of an impromptu river. The idol had come unloosed from a set of Burma, and it meandered earnestly on its way, stopping sometimes to waddle and bump in the shallows with the other debris of the tide. The two refugees had found sanctuary along a scroll of curls on its bald forehead and seemed at first glance to be sightseers on an interesting bus-ride through the scene of the flood.

"Will you look at that, Monroe!" said Robby. "Look at those dames!"

Dragging their legs through sudden bogs, they made their way to the bank of the stream. Now they could see the women, looking a little scared but brightening at the prospect of rescue.

"We ought to let 'em drift out to the waste pipe," said Robby gallantly, "but DeMille needs that head next week."

He wouldn't have hurt a fly, though, and presently he was hip deep in the water, fishing for them with a pole and succeeding only in spinning it in a dizzy circle. Help arrived, and the impression quickly got around that one of them was very pretty, and then that they were people of importance. But they were just strays, and Robby waited disgustedly to give them hell while the thing was brought finally into control and beached.

"Put that head back!" he called up to them. "You think it's a souvenir?"

One of the women came sliding smoothly down the cheek of the idol, and Robby caught and set her on solid ground; the other one hesitated and then followed. Robby turned to Stahr for judgment.

"What'll we do with them, chief?"

Stahr did not answer. Smiling faintly at him from not four feet away was the face of his dead wife, identical even to the expression. Across the four feet of moonlight, the eyes he knew looked back at him, a curl blew a little on a familiar forehead; the smile lingered, changed a little according to pattern; the lips parted—the same. An awful fear went over him, and he wanted to cry aloud. Back from the still sour room, the muffled glide of the limousine hearse, the falling concealing flowers, from out there in the dark—here now warm and glowing. The river passed him in a rush, the great spotlights swooped and blinked—and then he heard another voice speak that was not Minna's voice.

"We're sorry," said the voice. "We followed a truck in through a gate."

A little crowd had gathered—electricians, grips, truckers, and Robby began to nip at them like a sheep dog.

". . . get the big pumps on the tanks on Stage 4 . . . put a cable around this head . . . raft it up on a couple of two by fours . . . get the water out of the jungle first, for Christ's sake . . . that big 'A' pipe, lay it down . . . all that stuff is plastic. . . ."

Stahr stood watching the two women as they threaded their way after a policeman toward an exit gate. Then he took a tentative step to see if the weakness had gone out of his knees. A loud tractor came bumping through the slush, and men began streaming by him—every second one glancing at him, smiling, speaking: "Hello, Monroe. . . . Hello, Mr. Stahr . . . wet night, Mr. Stahr . . . Monroe . . . Monroe . . . Stahr . . . Stahr . . . Stahr."

He spoke and waved back as the people streamed by in the darkness, looking, I suppose, a little like the Emperor and the Old Guard. There is no world so but it has its heroes, and Stahr was the hero. Most of these men had been here a long time—through the beginnings and the great upset, when sound came, and the three years of depression, he had seen that no harm came to them. The old loyalties were trembling now, there were clay feet everywhere; but still he was their man, the last of the princes. And their greeting was a sort of low cheer as they went by.

CHAPTER III

BETWEEN THE NIGHT I got back and the quake, I'd made many observations.

About Father, for example. I loved Father—in a sort of irregular graph with many low swoops—but I began to see that his strong will didn't fill him out as a passable man. Most of what he accomplished boiled down to shrewd. He had acquired with luck and shrewdness a quarter interest in a booming circus—together with young Stahr. That was his life's effort—all the rest was an instinct to hang on. Of course, he talked that double talk to Wall Street about how mysterious it was to make a picture, but Father didn't know the ABC's of dubbing or even cutting. Nor had he learned much about the feel of America as a bar boy in Ballyhegan, nor did he have any more than a drummer's sense of a story. On the other hand, he didn't have concealed paresis like ———; he came to the studio before noon, and, with a suspiciousness developed like a muscle, it was hard to put anything over on him.

Stahr had been his luck—and Stahr was something else again. He was a marker in industry like Edison and Lumière and Griffith and Chaplin. He led pictures way up past the range and power of the theatre, reaching a sort of golden age, before the censorship.

Proof of his leadership was the spying that went on around him —not just for inside information or patented process secrets—but spying on his scent for a trend in taste, his guess as to how things were going to be. Too much of his vitality was taken by the mere parrying of these attempts. It made his work secret in part, often devious, slow—and hard to describe as the plans of a general, where the psychological factors become too tenuous and we end by merely adding up the successes and failures. But I have determined to give you a glimpse of him functioning, which is my excuse for what follows. It is drawn partly from a paper I wrote in college on *A*

28

Producer's Day and partly from my imagination. More often I have blocked in the ordinary events myself, while the stranger ones are true.

In the early morning after the flood, a man walked up to the outside balcony of the Administration Building. He lingered there some time, according to an eyewitness, then mounted to the iron railing and dove head first to the pavement below. Breakage—one arm.

Miss Doolan, Stahr's secretary, told him about it when he buzzed for her at nine. He had slept in his office without hearing the small commotion.

"Pete Zavras!" Stahr exclaimed, "—the camera man?"

"They took him to a doctor's office. It won't be in the paper."

"Hell of a thing," he said. "I knew he'd gone to pot—but I don't know why. He was all right when we used him two years ago—why should he come here? How did he get in?"

"He bluffed it with his old studio pass," said Catherine Doolan. She was a dry hawk, the wife of an assistant director. "Perhaps the quake had something to do with it."

"He was the best camera man in town," Stahr said. When he had heard of the hundreds dead at Long Beach, he was still haunted by the abortive suicide at dawn. He told Catherine Doolan to trace the matter down.

The first dictograph messages blew in through the warm morning. While he shaved and had coffee, he talked and listened. Robby had left a message: "If Mr. Stahr wants me tell him to hell with it I'm in bed." An actor was sick or thought so; the Governor of California was bringing a party out; a supervisor had beaten up his wife for the prints and must be "reduced to a writer"—these three affairs were Father's job—unless the actor was under personal contract to Stahr. There was early snow on a location in Canada with the company already there—Stahr raced over the possibilities of salvage, reviewing the story of the picture. Nothing. Stahr called Catherine Doolan.

"I want to speak to the cop who put two women off the back lot last night. I think his name's Malone."

"Yes, Mr. Stahr. I've got Joe Wyman—about the trousers."

"Hello, Joe," said Stahr. "Listen—two people at the sneak preview complained that Morgan's fly was open for half the picture . . . of course they're exaggerating, but even if it's only ten feet . . . no, we can't find the people, but I want that picture run over and over until you find that footage. Get a lot of people in the projection room—somebody'll spot it."

> *"Tout passe.—L'art robuste*
> *Seul a l'éternité."*

"And there's the Prince from Denmark," said Catherine Doolan. "He's very handsome." She was impelled to add pointlessly, "—for a tall man."

"Thanks," Stahr said. "Thank you, Catherine, I appreciate it that I am now the handsomest small man on the lot. Send the Prince out on the sets and tell him we'll lunch at one."

"And Mr. George Boxley—looking very angry in a British way."

"I'll see him for ten minutes."

As she went out, he asked: "Did Robby phone in?"

"No."

"Call sound, and if he's been heard from, call him and ask him this. Ask him this—did he hear that woman's name last night? Either of those women. Or anything so they could be traced."

"Anything else?"

"No, but tell him it's important while he still remembers. What were they? I mean what kind of people—ask him that, too. I mean were they——"

She waited, scratching his words on her pad without looking.

"—oh, were they—questionable? Were they theatrical? Never mind—skip that. Just ask if he knows how they can be traced."

The policeman, Malone, had known nothing. Two dames, and he had hustled 'em, you betcha. One of them was sore. Which one? One of them. They had a car, a Chevy—he thought of taking the license. Was it—the good looker who was sore? It was one of them.

Not which one—he had noticed nothing. Even on the lot here Minna was forgotten. In three years. So much for that, then.

Stahr smiled at Mr. George Boxley. It was a kindly fatherly smile Stahr had developed inversely when he was a young man pushed into high places. Originally it had been a smile of respect toward his elders, then as his own decisions grew rapidly to displace theirs, a smile so that they should not feel it—finally emerging as what it was: a smile of kindness—sometimes a little hurried and tired, but always there—toward anyone who had not angered him within the hour. Or anyone he did not intend to insult, aggressive and outright.

Mr. Boxley did not smile back. He came in with the air of being violently dragged, though no one apparently had a hand on him. He stood in front of a chair, and again it was as if two invisible attendants seized his arms and set him down forcibly into it. He sat there morosely. Even when he lit a cigarette on Stahr's invitation, one felt that the match was held to it by exterior forces he disdained to control.

Stahr looked at him courteously.

"Something not going well, Mr. Boxley?"

The novelist looked back at him in thunderous silence.

"I read your letter," said Stahr. The tone of the pleasant young headmaster was gone. He spoke as to an equal, but with a faint two-edged deference.

"I can't get what I write on paper," broke out Boxley. "You've all been very decent, but it's a sort of conspiracy. Those two hacks you've teamed me with listen to what I say, but they spoil it—they seem to have a vocabulary of about a hundred words."

"Why don't you write it yourself?" asked Stahr.

"I have. I sent you some."

"But it was just talk, back and forth," said Stahr mildly. "Interesting talk but nothing more."

Now it was all the two ghostly attendants could do to hold Boxley in the deep chair. He struggled to get up; he uttered a single quiet bark which had some relation to laughter but none to amusement, and said:

"I don't think you people read things. The men are duelling when the conversation takes place. At the end one of them falls into a well and has to be hauled up in a bucket."

He barked again and subsided.

"Would you write that in a book of your own, Mr. Boxley?"

"What? Naturally not."

"You'd consider it too cheap."

Movie standards are different," said Boxley, hedging.

"Do you ever go to them?"

"No—almost never."

"Isn't it because people are always duelling and falling down wells?"

"Yes—and wearing strained facial expressions and talking incredible and unnatural dialogue."

"Skip the dialogue for a minute," said Stahr. "Granted your dialogue is more graceful than what these hacks can write—that's why we brought you out here. But let's imagine something that isn't either bad dialogue or jumping down a well. Has your office got a stove in it that lights with a match?"

"I think it has," said Boxley stiffly, "—but I never use it."

"Suppose you're in your office. You've been fighting duels or writing all day and you're too tired to fight or write any more. You're sitting there staring—dull, like we all get sometimes. A pretty stenographer that you've seen before comes into the room and you watch her—idly. She doesn't see you, though you're very close to her. She takes off her gloves, opens her purse and dumps it out on a table——"

Stahr stood up, tossing his key-ring on his desk.

"She has two dimes and a nickel—and a cardboard match box. She leaves the nickel on the desk, puts the two dimes back into her purse and takes her black gloves to the stove, opens it and puts them inside. There is one match in the match box and she starts to light it kneeling by the stove. You notice that there's a stiff wind blowing in the window—but just then your telephone rings. The girl picks it up, says hello—listens—and says deliberately into the phone, 'I've never owned a pair of black gloves in my life.' She hangs up, kneels by the stove again, and just as she lights the match, you glance around very suddenly and see that there's another man in the office, watching every move the girl makes——"

Stahr paused. He picked up his keys and put them in his pocket.

"Go on," said Boxley smiling. "What happens?"

"I don't know," said Stahr. "I was just making pictures."

Boxley felt he was being put in the wrong.

"It's just melodrama," he said.

"Not necessarily," said Stahr. "In any case, nobody has moved violently or talked cheap dialogue or had any facial expression at all. There was only one bad line, and a writer like you could improve it. But you were interested."

"What was the nickel for?" asked Boxley evasively.

"I don't know," said Stahr. Suddenly he laughed. "Oh, yes—the nickel was for the movies."

The two invisible attendants seemed to release Boxley. He relaxed, leaned back in his chair and laughed.

"What in hell do you pay me for?" he demanded. "I don't understand the damn stuff."

"You will," said Stahr grinning, "or you wouldn't have asked about the nickel."

A dark saucer-eyed man was waiting in the outer office as they came out.

"Mr. Boxley, this is Mr. Mike Van Dyke," Stahr said. "What is it, Mike?"

"Nothing," Mike said. "I just came up to see if you were real."

"Why don't you go to work?" Stahr said. "I haven't had a laugh in the rushes for days."

"I'm afraid of a nervous breakdown."

"You ought to keep in form," Stahr said. "Let's see you peddle your stuff." He turned to Boxley: "Mike's a gag man—he was out here when I was in the cradle. Mike, show Mr. Boxley a double wing, clutch, kick and scram."

"Here?" asked Mike.

"Here."

"There isn't much room. I wanted to ask you about——"

"There's lot of room."

"Well," he looked around tentatively. "You shoot the gun."

Miss Doolan's assistant, Katy, took a paper bag, blew it open.

"It was a routine," Mike said to Boxley, "—back in the Keystone days." He turned to Stahr: "Does he know what a routine is?"

"It means an act," Stahr explained. "Georgie Jessel talks about 'Lincoln's Gettysburg routine.'"

Katy poised the neck of the blown-up bag in her mouth. Mike stood with his back to her.

"Ready?" Katy asked. She brought her hands down on the side. Immediately Mike grabbed his bottom with both hands, jumped in the air, slid his feet out on the floor one after the other, remaining in place and flapping his arms twice like a bird——

"Double wing," said Stahr.

—and then ran out the screen door which the office boy held open for him and disappeared past the window of the balcony.

"Mr. Stahr," said Miss Doolan, "Mr. Hanson is on the phone from New York."

Ten minutes later he clicked his dictograph, and Miss Doolan came in. There was a male star waiting to see him in the outer office, Miss Doolan said.

"Tell him I went out by the balcony," Stahr advised her.

"All right. He's been in four times this week. He seems very anxious."

"Did he give you any hint of what he wanted? Isn't it something he can see Mr. Brady about?"

"He didn't say. You have a conference coming up. Miss Meloney and Mr. White are outside. Mr. Broaca is next door in Mr. Reinmund's office."

"Send Mr. Roderiguez in," said Stahr. "Tell him I can see him only for a minute."

When the handsome actor came in, Stahr remained standing.

"What is it that can't wait?" he asked pleasantly.

The actor waited carefully till Miss Doolan had gone out.

"Monroe, I'm through," he said. "I had to see you."

"Through!" said Stahr. "Have you seen *Variety*? Your picture's held over at Roxy's and did thirty-seven thousand in Chicago last week."

"That's the worst of it. That's the tragedy. I get everything I want, and now it means nothing."

"Well, go on, explain."

"There's nothing between Esther and me any more. There never can be again."

"A row."

"Oh, no—worse—I can't bear to mention it. My head's in a daze. I wander around like a madman. I go through my part as if I was asleep."

"I haven't noticed it," said Stahr. "You were great in your rushes yesterday."

"Was I? That just shows you nobody ever guesses."

"Are you trying to tell me that you and Esther are separating?"

"I suppose it'll come to that. Yes—inevitably—it will."

"What was it?" demanded Stahr impatiently. "Did she come in without knocking?"

"Oh, there's nobody else. It's just—me. I'm through."

Stahr got it suddenly.

"How do you know?"

"It's been true for six weeks."

"It's your imagination," said Stahr. "Have you been to a doctor?"

The actor nodded.

"I've tried everything. I even—one day in desperation I went down to—to Claris. But it was hopeless. I'm washed up."

Stahr had an impish temptation to tell him to go to Brady about it. Brady handled all matters of public relations. Or was this private relations. He turned away a moment, got his face in control, turned back.

"I've been to Pat Brady," said the star, as if guessing the thought. "He gave me a lot of phoney advice and I tried it all, but nothing doing. Esther and I sit opposite each other at dinner, and I'm ashamed to look at her. She's been a good sport about it, but I'm ashamed. I'm ashamed all day long. I think *Rainy Day* grossed twenty-five thousand in Des Moines and broke all records in St. Louis and did twenty-seven thousand in Kansas City. My fan mail's way up, and there I am afraid to go home at night, afraid to go to bed."

Stahr began to be faintly oppressed. When the actor first came in, Stahr had intended to invite him to a cocktail party, but now it scarcely seemed appropriate. What would he want with a cocktail party with this hanging over him? In his mind's eye he saw him wandering haunted from guest to guest with a cocktail in his hand and his grosses up twenty-seven thousand.

"So I came to you, Monroe. I never saw a situation where you didn't know a way out. I said to myself: even if he advises me to kill myself, I'll ask Monroe."

The buzzer sounded on Stahr's desk—he switched on the dictograph and heard Miss Doolan's voice.

"Five minutes, Mr. Stahr."

"I'm sorry," said Stahr. "I'll need a few minutes more."

"Five hundred girls marched to my house from the high school," the actor said gloomily, "and I stood behind the curtains and watched them. I couldn't go out."

"You sit down," said Stahr. "We'll take plenty of time and talk this over."

In the outer office, two members of the conference group had already waited ten minutes—Wylie White and Jane Meloney. The latter was a dried-up little blonde of fifty about whom one could hear the fifty assorted opinions of Hollywood—"a sentimental dope," "the best writer on construction in Hollywood," "a veteran," "that old hack," "the smartest woman on the lot," "the cleverest plagiarist in the biz"; and, of course, in addition she was variously described as a nymphomaniac, a virgin, a pushover, a Lesbian and a faithful wife. Without being an old maid, she was, like most self-made women, rather old maidish. She had ulcers of the stomach, and her salary was over a hundred thousand a year. A complicated treatise could be written on whether she was "worth it" or more than that or nothing at all. Her value lay in such ordinary assets as the bare fact that she was a woman and adaptable, quick and trustworthy, "knew the game" and was without egotism. She had been a great friend of Minna's, and over a period of years Stahr had managed to stifle what amounted to a sharp physical revulsion.

She and Wylie waited in silence—occasionally addressing a remark to Miss Doolan. Every few minutes Reinmund, the supervisor, called up from his office, where he and Broaca, the director, were waiting. After ten minutes Stahr's button went on, and Miss Doolan called Reinmund and Broaca; simultaneously Stahr and the actor came out of Stahr's office with Stahr holding the man's arm. He was so wound up now that when Wylie White asked him how he was he opened his mouth and began to tell him then and there.

"Oh, I've had an awful time," he said, but Stahr interrupted sharply.

"No, you haven't. Now you go along and do the role the way I said."

"Thank you, Monroe."

Jane Meloney looked after him without speaking.

"Somebody been catching flies on him?" she asked—a phrase for stealing scenes.

"I'm sorry I kept you waiting," Stahr said. "Come on in."

It was noon already and the conferees were entitled to exactly an hour of Stahr's time. No less, for such a conference could only be interrupted by a director who was held up in his shooting; seldom much more, because every eight days the company must release a production as complex and costly as Reinhardt's *Miracle*.

Occasionally, less often than five years ago, Stahr would work all through the night on a single picture. But after such a spree he felt badly for days. If he could go from problem to problem, there was a certain rebirth of vitality with each change. And like those sleepers who can wake whenever they wish, he had set his psychological clock to run one hour.

The cast assembled included, besides the writers, Reinmund, one of the most favored of the supervisors, and John Broaca, the picture's director.

Broaca, on the surface, was all engineer—large and without nerves, quietly resolute, popular. He was an ignoramus, and Stahr often caught him making the same scenes over and over—one scene about a rich young girl occurred in all his pictures with the same action, the same business. A bunch of large dogs entered the room and jumped around the girl. Later the girl went to a stable and slapped a horse on the rump. The explanation was probably not Freudian; more likely that at a drab moment in youth he had looked through a fence and seen a beautiful girl with dogs and horses. As a trademark for glamor it was stamped on his brain forever.

Reinmund was a handsome young opportunist, with a fairly good education. Originally a man of some character, he was being daily forced by his anomalous position into devious ways of acting and thinking. He was a bad man now, as men go. At thirty he had none of the virtues which either gentile Americans or Jews are taught to think admirable. But he got his pictures out in time, and by manifesting an almost homosexual fixation on Stahr, seemed to have dulled Stahr's usual acuteness. Stahr liked him—considered him a good all-around man.

Wylie White, of course, in any country would have been recognizable as an intellectual of the second order. He was civilized and voluble, both simple and acute, half dazed and half saturnine. His jealousy of Stahr showed only in unguarded flashes, and was mingled with admiration and even affection.

"The production date for this picture is two weeks from Saturday," said Stahr. "I think basically it's all right—much improved."

Reinmund and the two writers exchanged a glance of congratulation.

"Except for one thing," said Stahr, thoughtfully. "I don't see why it should be produced at all, and I've decided to put it away."

There was a moment of shocked silence—and then murmurs of protest, stricken queries.

"It's not your fault," Stahr said. "I thought there was something there that wasn't there—that was all." He hesitated, looking regretfully at Reinmund: "It's too bad—it was a good play. We paid fifty thousand for it."

"What's the matter with it, Monroe?" asked Broaca bluntly.

"Well, it hardly seems worth while to go into it," said Stahr.

Reinmund and Wylie White were both thinking of the professional effect on them. Reinmund had two pictures to his account this year—but Wylie White needed a credit to start his comeback to the scene. Jane Meloney was watching Stahr closely from little skull-like eyes.

"Couldn't you give us some clue," Reinmund asked. "This is a good deal of a blow, Monroe."

"I just wouldn't put Margaret Sullavan in it," said Stahr. "Or Colman either. I wouldn't advise them to play it——"

"Specifically, Monroe," begged Wylie White. "What didn't you like? The scenes? the dialogue? the humor? construction?"

Stahr picked up the script from his desk, let it fall as if it were, physically, too heavy to handle.

"I don't like the people," he said. "I wouldn't like to meet them —if I knew they were going to be somewhere, I'd go somewhere else."

Reinmund smiled, but there was worry in his eyes.

"Well, that's a damning criticism," he said. "I thought the people were rather interesting."

"So did I," said Broaca. "I thought Em was very sympathetic."

"Did you?" asked Stahr sharply. "I could just barely believe she was alive. And when I came to the end, I said to myself, 'So what?'"

"There must be something to do," Reinmund said. "Naturally we feel bad about this. This is the structure we agreed on——"

"But it's not the story," said Stahr. "I've told you many times that the first thing I decide is the *kind* of story I want. We change in every other regard, but once that is set we've got to work toward it with every line and movement. This is not the kind of a story I want. The story we bought had shine and glow—it was a happy story. This is all full of doubt and hesitation. The hero and heroine stop loving each other over trifles—then they start up again over trifles. After the first sequence, you don't care if she never sees him again or he her."

"That's my fault," said Wylie suddenly. "You see, Monroe, I don't think stenographers have the same dumb admiration for their bosses they had in 1929. They've been laid off—they've seen their bosses jittery. The world has moved on, that's all."

Stahr looked at him impatiently, gave a short nod.

"That's not under discussion," he said. "The premise of this story is that the girl did have dumb admiration for her boss, if you want to call it that. And there wasn't any evidence that he'd ever been jittery. When you make her doubt him in any way, you have a different kind of story. Or rather you haven't anything at all. These people are extraverts—get that straight—and I want them to extravert all over the lot. When I want to do a Eugene O'Neill play, I'll buy one."

Jane Meloney, who had never taken her eyes off Stahr, knew it was going to be all right now. If he had really been going to abandon the picture, he wouldn't have gone at it like this. She had been in this game longer than any of them except Broaca, with whom she had had a three-day affair twenty years ago.

Stahr turned to Reinmund.

"You ought to have understood from the casting, Reiny, what kind of a picture I wanted. I started marking the lines that Corliss and McKelway couldn't say and got tired of it. Remember this in the future—if I order a limousine, I want that kind of car. And the fastest midget racer you ever saw wouldn't do. Now—" He looked around. "—shall we go any farther? Now that I've told you I don't even like the kind of picture this is? Shall we go on? We've got two weeks. At the end of that time I'm going to put Corliss and McKelway into this or something else—is it worth while?"

"Well, naturally," said Reinmund, "I think it is. I feel bad about this. I should have warned Wylie. I thought he had some good ideas."

"Monroe's right," said Broaca bluntly. "I felt this was wrong all the time, but I couldn't put my finger on it."

Wylie and Jane looked at him contemptuously and exchanged a glance.

"Do you writers think you can get hot on it again?" asked Stahr, not unkindly. "Or shall I try somebody fresh?"

"I'd like another shot," said Wylie.

"How about you, Jane?"

She nodded briefly.

"What do you think of the girl?" asked Stahr.

"Well—naturally I'm prejudiced in her favor."

"You better forget it," said Stahr warningly. "Ten million Americans would put thumbs down on that girl if she walked on the screen. We've got an hour and twenty-five minutes on the screen —you show a woman being unfaithful to a man for one-third of that time and you've given the impression that she's one-third whore."

"Is that a big proportion?" asked Jane slyly, and they laughed.

"It is for me," said Stahr thoughtfully, "even if it wasn't for the Hays office. If you want to paint a scarlet letter on her back, it's all right, but that's another story. Not this story. This is a future wife and mother. However—*however*——"

He pointed his pencil at Wylie White.

"—this has as much passion as that Oscar on my desk."

"What the hell!" said Wylie. "She's full of it. Why she goes to——"

"She's loose enough," said Stahr, "—but that's all. There's one scene in the play better than all this you cooked up, and you've left it out. When she's trying to make the time pass by changing her watch."

"It didn't seem to fit," Wylie apologized.

"Now," said Stahr, "I've got about fifty ideas. I'm going to call

Miss Doolan." He pressed a button. "—And if there's anything you don't understand, speak up——"

Miss Doolan slid in almost imperceptibly. Pacing the floor swiftly, Stahr began. In the first place he wanted to tell them what kind of a girl she was—what kind of a girl he approved of here. She was a perfect girl with a few small faults as in the play, but a perfect girl not because the public wanted her that way but because it was the kind of girl that he, Stahr, liked to see in this sort of picture. Was that clear? It was no character role. She stood for health, vitality, ambition and love. What gave the play its importance was entirely a situation in which she found herself. She became possessed of a secret that affected a great many lives. There was a right thing and a wrong thing to do—at first it was not plain which was which, but when it was, she went right away and did it. That was the kind of story this was—thin, clean and shining. No doubts.

"She has never heard the word labor troubles," he said with a sigh. "She might be living in 1929. Is it plain what kind of girl I want?"

"It's very plain, Monroe."

"Now about the things she does," said Stahr. "At all times, at all moments when she is on the screen in our sight, she wants to sleep with Ken Willard. Is that plain, Wylie?"

"Passionately plain."

"Whatever she does, it is in place of sleeping with Ken Willard. If she walks down the street she is walking to sleep with Ken Willard, if she eats her food it is to give her strength to sleep with Ken Willard. *But* at no time do you give the impression that she would ever consider sleeping with Ken Willard unless they were properly sanctified. I'm ashamed of having to tell you these kindergarten facts, but they have somehow leaked out of the story."

He opened the script and began to go through it page by page. Miss Doolan's notes would be typed in quintuplicate and given to them, but Jane Meloney made notes of her own. Broaca put his hand up to his half-closed eyes—he could remember "when a director was something out here," when writers were gag-men or eager and ashamed young reporters full of whiskey—a director was all there was then. No supervisor—no Stahr.

He started wide-awake as he heard his name.

"It would be nice, John, if you could put the boy on a pointed roof and let him walk around and keep the camera on him. You might get a nice feeling—not danger, not suspense, not pointing for anything—a kid on the roof in the morning."

Broaca brought himself back in the room.

"All right," he said, "—just an element of danger."

"Not exactly," said Stahr. "He doesn't start to fall off the roof. Break into the next scene with it."

"Through the window," suggested Jane Meloney. "He could climb in his sister's window."

"That's a good transition," said Stahr. "Right into the diary scene."

Broaca was wide-awake now.

"I'll shoot up at him," he said. "Let him go away from the camera. Just a fixed shot from quite a distance—let him go away from the camera. Don't follow him. Pick him up in a close shot and let him go away again. No attention on him except against the whole roof and the sky." He liked the shot—it was a director's shot that didn't come up on every page any more. He might use a crane—it would be cheaper in the end than building the roof on the ground with a process sky. That was one thing about Stahr—the literal sky was the limit. He had worked with Jews too long to believe legends that they were small with money.

"In the third sequence have him hit the priest," Stahr said.

"What!" Wylie cried, "—and have the Catholics on our neck."

"I've talked to Joe Breen. Priests have been hit. It doesn't reflect on them."

His quiet voice ran on—stopped abruptly as Miss Doolan glanced at the clock.

"Is that too much to do before Monday?" he asked Wylie.

Wylie looked at Jane and she looked back, not even bothering to nod. He saw their week-end melting away, but he was a different man from when he entered the room. When you were paid fifteen hundred a week, emergency work was one thing you did not skimp, nor when your picture was threatened. As a "free lance" writer Wylie had failed from lack of caring, but here was Stahr to care, for all of them. The effect would not wear off when he left the office—not anywhere within the walls of the lot. He felt a great purposefulness. The mixture of common sense, wise sensibility, theatrical ingenuity, and a certain half-naïve conception of the common weal which Stahr had just stated aloud, inspired him to do his part, to get his block of stone in place, even if the effort were fore-doomed, the result as dull as a pyramid.

Out of the window Jane Meloney watched the trickle streaming toward the commissary. She would have her lunch in her office and knit a few rows while it came. The man was coming at one-fifteen with the French perfume smuggled over the Mexican border. That was no sin—it was like prohibition.

Broaca watched as Reinmund fawned upon Stahr. He sensed that Reinmund was on his way up. He received seven hundred and fifty a week for his partial authority over directors, writers and stars who got much more. He wore a pair of cheap English shoes he had bought near the Beverly Wilshire, and Broaca hoped they hurt his feet, but soon now he would order his shoes from Peel's and put away his little green Alpine hat with a feather. Broaca was years ahead of him. He had a fine record in the war, but he had never felt quite the same with himself since he had let Ike Franklin strike him in the face with his open hand.

There was smoke in the room, and behind it, behind his great desk, Stahr was withdrawing further and further, in all courtesy, still giving Reinmund an ear and Miss Doolan an ear. The conference was over.

[*Stahr was to have received the Danish Prince Agge, who "wanted to learn about pictures from the beginning" and who in the author's cast of characters is described as an "early Fascist."*]

"Mr. Marcus calling from New York," said Miss Doolan.

"What do you mean?" demanded Stahr. "Why, I saw him here last night."

"Well, he's on the phone—it's a New York call and Miss Jacobs' voice. It's his office."

Stahr laughed.

"I'm seeing him at lunch," he said. "There's no aeroplane fast enough to take him there."

Miss Doolan returned to the phone. Stahr lingered to hear the outcome.

"It's all right," said Miss Doolan presently. "It was a mistake. Mr. Marcus called East this morning to tell them about the quake and the flood on the back lot, and it seems he asked them to ask you about it. It was a new secretary who didn't understand Mr. Marcus. I think she got mixed up."

"I think she did," said Stahr grimly.

Prince Agge did not understand either of them, but, looking for the fabulous, he felt it was something triumphantly American. Mr. Marcus, whose quarters could be seen across the way, had called his New York office to ask Stahr about the flood. The Prince imagined some intricate relationship without realizing that the transaction had taken place entirely within the once brilliant steel-trap mind of Mr. Marcus, which was intermittently slipping.

"I think she was a very new secretary," repeated Stahr. "Any other messages?"

"Mr. Robinson called in," Miss Doolan said, as he started for the commissary. "One of the women told him her name, but he's forgotten it—he thinks it was Smith or Brown or Jones."

"That's a great help."

"And he remembers she says she just moved to Los Angeles."

"I remember she had a silver belt," Stahr said, "with stars cut out of it."

"I'm still trying to find out more about Pete Zavras. I talked to his wife."

"What did she say?"

"Oh, they've had an awful time—given up their house—she's been sick——"

"Is the eye-trouble hopeless?"

"She didn't seem to know anything about the state of his eyes. She didn't even know he was going blind."

"That's funny."

He thought about it on the way to luncheon, but it was as confusing as the actor's trouble this morning. Troubles about people's health didn't seem within his range—he gave no thought to his own. In the lane beside the commissary he stepped back as an open electric truck crammed with girls in the bright costumes of the

Regency came rolling in from the back lot. The dresses were fluttering in the wind, the young painted faces looked at him curiously, and he smiled as it went by.

Eleven men and their guest, Prince Agge, sat at lunch in the private dining room of the studio commissary. They were the money men—they were the rulers; and unless there was a guest, they ate in broken silence, sometimes asking questions about each other's wives and children, sometimes discharging a single absorption from the forefront of their consciousness. Eight out of the ten were Jews—five of the ten were foreign-born, including a Greek and an Englishman; and they had all known each other for a long time: there was a rating in the group, from old Marcus down to old Leanbaum, who had bought the most fortunate block of stock in the business and never was allowed to spend over a million a year producing.

Old Marcus still managed to function with disquieting resilience. Some never-atrophying instinct warned him of danger, of gangings up against him—he was never so dangerous himself as when others considered him surrounded. His grey face had attained such immobility that even those who were accustomed to watch the reflex of the inner corner of his eye could no longer see it. Nature had grown a little white whisker there to conceal it; his armor was complete.

As he was the oldest, Stahr was the youngest of the group—not by many years at this date, though he had first sat with most of these men when he was a boy wonder of twenty-two. Then, more than now, he had been a money man among money men. Then he had been able to figure costs in his head with a speed and accuracy that dazzled them—for they were not wizards or even experts in that regard, despite the popular conception of Jews in finance. Most of them owed their success to different and incompatible qualities. But in a group a tradition carries along the less adept, and they were content to look at Stahr for the sublimated auditing, and experience a sort of glow as if they had done it themselves, like rooters at a football game.

Stahr, as will presently be seen, had grown away from that particular gift, though it was always there.

Prince Agge sat between Stahr and Mort Fleishacker, the com-

pany lawyer, and across from Joe Popolos the theatre owner. He was
hostile to Jews in a vague general way that he tried to cure himself
of. As a turbulent man, serving his time in the Foreign Legion, he
thought that Jews were too fond of their own skins. But he was will-
ing to concede that they might be different in America under different circumstances, and certainly he found Stahr was much of a
man in every way. For the rest—he thought most business men were
dull dogs—for final reference he reverted always to the blood of
Bernadotte in his veins.

My father—I will call him Mr. Brady, as Prince Agge did when
he told me of this luncheon—was worried about a picture, and
when Leanbaum went out early, he came up and took his chair
opposite.

"How about the South America picture idea, Monroe?" he asked.

Prince Agge noticed a blink of attention toward them as distinct
as if a dozen pairs of eyelashes had made the sound of batting wings.
Then silence again.

"We're going ahead with it," said Stahr.

"With that same budget?" Brady asked.

Stahr nodded.

"It's out of proportion," said Brady. "There won't be any miracle
in these bad times—no *Hell's Angels* or *Ben Hur,* when you throw
it away and get it back."

Probably the attack was planned, for Popolos, the Greek, took up
the matter in a sort of double talk.

"It's not adoptable, Monroe, in as we wish adopt to this times in
as it changes. It what could be done as we run the gamut of pros-
perity is scarcely conceptuable now."

"What do you think, Mr. Marcus?" asked Stahr.

All eyes followed his down the table, but, as if forewarned, Mr.
Marcus had already signalled his private waiter behind him that
he wished to rise, and was even now in a basket-like position in the
waiter's arms. He looked at them with such helplessness that it was
hard to realize that in the evenings he sometimes went dancing
with his young Canadian girl.

"Monroe is our production genuis," he said. "I count upon Monroe and lean heavily upon him. I have not seen the flood myself."

There was a moment of silence as he moved from the room.

"There's not a two million dollar gross in the country now," said Brady.

"Is not," agreed Popolos. "Even as if so you could grab them by the head and push them by and in, is not."

"Probably not," agreed Stahr. He paused as if to make sure that all were listening. "I think we can count on a million and a quarter from the road-show. Perhaps a million and a half altogether. And a quarter of a million abroad."

Again there was silence—this time puzzled, a little confused. Over his shoulder Stahr asked the waiter to be connected with his office on the phone.

"But your budget?" said Fleishacker. "Your budget is seventeen hundred and fifty thousand, I understand. And your expectations only add up to that without profit."

"Those aren't my expectations," said Stahr. "We're not sure of more than a million and a half."

The room had grown so motionless that Prince Agge could hear a grey chunk of ash fall from a cigar in midair. Fleishacker started to speak, his face fixed with amazement, but a phone had been handed over Stahr's shoulder.

"Your office, Mr. Stahr."

"Oh, yes—oh, hello, Miss Doolan. I've figured it out about Zavras. It's one of these lousy rumors—I'll bet my shirt on it. . . . Oh, you did. Good. . . . good. Now here's what to do: send him to my oculist this afternoon—Dr. John Kennedy—and have him get a report and have it photostated—you understand?"

He hung up—turned with a touch of passion to the table at large.

"Did any of you ever hear a story that Pete Zavras was going blind?"

There were a couple of nods. But most of those present were poised breathlessly on whether Stahr had slipped on his figures a minute before.

"It's pure bunk. He says he's never even been to an oculist— never knew why the studios turned against him," said Stahr. "Somebody didn't like him or somebody talked too much, and he's been out of work for a year."

There was a conventional murmur of sympathy. Stahr signed the check and made as though to get up.

"Excuse me, Monroe," said Fleishacker persistently, while Brady and Popolos watched. "I'm fairly new here, and perhaps I fail to comprehend implicitly and explicitly." He was talking fast, but the veins on his forehead bulged with pride at the big words from N. Y. U. "Do I understand you to say you expect to gross a quarter million short of your budget?"

"It's a quality picture," said Stahr with assumed innocence.

It had dawned on them all now, but they still felt there was a trick in it. Stahr really thought it would make money. No one in his senses——

"For two years we've played safe," said Stahr. "It's time we made a picture that'll lose some money. Write it off as good will—this'll bring in new customers."

Some of them still thought he meant it was a flyer and a favorable one, but he left them in no doubt.

"It'll lose money," he said as he stood up, his jaw just slightly out and his eyes smiling and shining. "It would be a bigger miracle than *Hell's Angels* if it broke even. But we have a certain duty to the public, as Pat Brady has said at Academy dinners. It's a good thing for the production schedule to slip in a picture that'll lose money."

He nodded at Prince Agge. As the latter made his bows quickly, he tried to take in with a last glance the general effect of what Stahr said, but he could tell nothing. The eyes, not so much downcast as fixed upon an indefinite distance just above the table, were all blinking quickly now, but there was not a whisper in the room.

Coming out of the private dining room, they passed through a corner of the commissary proper. Prince Agge drank it in—eagerly. It was gay with gypsies and with citizens and soldiers, with the sideburns and braided coats of the First Empire. From a little distance they were men who lived and walked a hundred years ago, and Agge wondered how he and the men of his time would look as extras in some future costume picture.

Then he saw Abraham Lincoln, and his whole feeling suddenly changed. He had been brought up in the dawn of Scandinavian socialism when Nicolay's biography was much read. He had been told Lincoln was a great man whom he should admire, and he hated him instead, because he was forced upon him. But now seeing him sitting here, his legs crossed, his kindly face fixed on a forty-cent dinner, including dessert, his shawl wrapped around him as if to protect himself from the erratic air-cooling—now Prince Agge, who was in America at last, stared as a tourist at the mummy of Lenin in the Kremlin. This, then, was Lincoln. Stahr had walked on far ahead of him, turned waiting for him—but still Agge stared.

This, then, he thought, was what they all meant to be.

Lincoln suddenly raised a triangle of pie and jammed it in his mouth, and, a little frightened, Prince Agge hurried to join Stahr.

"I hope you're getting what you want," said Stahr, feeling he had neglected him. "We'll have some rushes in half an hour and then you can go on to as many sets as you want."

"I should rather stay with you," said Prince Agge.

"I'll see what there is for me," said Stahr. "Then we'll go on together."

There was the Japanese consul on the release of a spy story which might offend the national sensibilities of Japan. There were phone calls and telegrams. There was some further information from Robby.

"Now he remembers the name of the woman. He's sure it was Smith," said Miss Doolan. "He asked her if she wanted to come on the lot and get some dry shoes, and she said no—so she can't sue."

"That's pretty bad for a total recall—'Smith.' That's a great help." He thought a moment: "Ask the phone company for a list of Smiths that have taken new phones here in the last month. Call them all."

"All right."

CHAPTER IV

"How ARE YOU, Monroe," said Red Ridingwood. "I'm glad you came down."

Stahr walked past him, heading across the great stage toward the set of a brilliant room that would be used tomorrow. Director Ridingwood followed, realizing after a moment that, however fast he walked, Stahr managed to be a step or two ahead. He recognized the indication of displeasure—he had used it himself. He had had his own studio once and he had used everything. There was no stop Stahr could pull that would surprise him. His task was the delivery of situations, and Stahr by effective business could not outplay him on his own grounds. Goldwyn had once interfered with him, and Ridingwood had led Goldwyn into trying to act out a part in front of fifty people—with the result that he had anticipated: his own authority had been restored.

Stahr reached the brilliant set and stopped.

"It's no good," said Ridingwood. "No imagination. I don't care how you light it——"

"Why did you call me about it?" Stahr asked, standing close to him. "Why didn't you take it up with Art?"

"I didn't ask you to come down, Monroe."

"You wanted to be your own supervisor."

"I'm sorry, Monroe," said Ridingwood patiently, "but I didn't ask you to come down."

Stahr turned suddenly and walked back toward the camera set-up. The eyes and open mouths of a group of visitors moved momentarily off the heroine of the picture, took in Stahr, and then moved vacantly back to the heroine again. They were Knights of Columbus. They had seen the host carried in procession, but this was the dream made flesh.

Stahr stopped beside her chair. She wore a low gown which displayed the bright eczema of her chest and back. Before each take, the blemished surface was plastered over with an emollient, which was removed immediately after the take. Her hair was of the color and viscosity of drying blood, but there was starlight that actually photographed in her eyes.

Before Stahr could speak, he heard a helpful voice behind him: "She's radiunt. Absolutely radiunt."

It was an assistant director, and the intention was delicate compliment. The actress was being complimented so that she did not have to strain her poor skin to bend and hear. Stahr was being complimented for having her under contract. Ridingwood was being remotely complimented.

"Everything all right?" Stahr asked her pleasantly.

"Oh, it's fine," she agreed, "—except for the ——ing publicity men."

He winked at her gently.

"We'll keep them away," he said.

Her name had become currently synonymous with the expression "bitch." Presumably she had modelled herself after one of those queens in the Tarzan comics who rule mysteriously over a nation of blacks. She regarded the rest of the world as black. She was a necessary evil, borrowed for a single picture.

Ridingwood walked with Stahr toward the door of the stage.

"Everything's all right," the director said. "She's as good as she can be."

They were out of hearing range, and Stahr stopped suddenly and looked at Red with blazing eyes.

"You've been photographing crap," he said. "Do you know what she reminds me of in the rushes—'Miss Foodstuffs.'"

"I'm trying to get the best performance——"

"Come along with me," said Stahr abruptly.

"With you? Shall I tell them to rest?"

"Leave it as it is," said Stahr, pushing the padded outer door.

His car and chauffeur waited outside. Minutes were precious most days.

"Get in," said Stahr.

Red knew now it was serious. He even knew all at once what was the matter. The girl had got the whip hand on him tne first day with her cold lashing tongue. He was a peace-loving man and he had let her walk through her part cold rather than cause trouble.

Stahr spoke into his thoughts.

"You can't handle her," he said. "I told you what I wanted. I wanted her *mean*—and she comes out bored. I'm afraid we'll have to call it off, Red."

"The picture?"

"No. I'm putting Harley on it."

"All right, Monroe."

"I'm sorry, Red. We'll try something else another time."

The car drew up in front of Stahr's office.

"Shall I finish this take?" said Red.

"It's being done now," said Stahr grimly. "Harley's in there."

"What the hell——"

"He went in when we came out. I had him read the script last night."

"Now listen, Monroe——"

"It's my busy day, Red," said Stahr, tersely. "You lost interest about three days ago."

It was a sorry mess, Ridingwood thought. It meant he would have slight, very slight loss of position—it probably meant that he could not have a third wife just now as he had planned. There wasn't even the satisfaction of raising a row about it—if you disagreed with Stahr, you did not advertise it. Stahr was his world's great customer, who was always—almost always—right.

"How about my coat?" he asked suddenly. "I left it over a chair on the set."

"I know you did," said Stahr. "Here it is."

He was trying so hard to be charitable about Ridingwood's lapse that he had forgotten that he had it in his hand.

"Mr. Stahr's Projection Room" was a miniature picture theatre with four rows of overstuffed chairs. In front of the front row ran long tables with dim lamps, buzzers and telephones. Against the wall was an upright piano, left there since the early days of sound. The room had been redecorated and reupholstered only a year before, but already it was ragged again with work and hours.

Here Stahr sat at two-thirty and again at six-thirty watching the lengths of film taken during the day. There was often a savage tensity about the occasion—he was dealing with *faits accomplis*— the net result of months of buying, planning, writing and rewriting, casting, constructing, lighting, rehearsing and shooting—the fruit of brilliant hunches or of counsels of despair, of lethargy, conspiracy and sweat. At this point the tortuous manœuvre was staged and in suspension—these were reports from the battle-line.

Besides Stahr, there were present the representatives of all technical departments, together with the supervisors and unit managers of the pictures concerned. The directors did not appear at these showings—officially because their work was considered done, actually because few punches were pulled here as money ran out in silver spools. There had evolved a delicate staying away.

The staff was already assembled. Stahr came in and took his place quickly, and the murmur of conversation died away. As he sat back and drew his thin knee up beside him in the chair, the lights in the room went out. There was the flare of a match in the back row—then silence.

On the screen a troop of French Canadians pushed their canoes up a rapids. The scene had been photographed in a studio tank, and at the end of each take, after the director's voice could be heard saying "Cut," the actors on the screen relaxed and wiped their brows and sometimes laughed hilariously—and the water in the tank stopped flowing and the illusion ceased. Except to name his choice from each set of takes and to remark that it was "a good process," Stahr made no comment.

The next scene, still in the rapids, called for dialogue between the Canadian girl (Claudette Colbert) and the *courrier du bois* (Ronald Colman), with her looking down at him from a canoe. After a few strips had run through, Stahr spoke up suddenly.

"Has the tank been dismantled?"

"Yes, sir."

"Monroe—they needed it for——"

Stahr cut in peremptorily.

"Have it set up again right away. Let's have that second take again."

The lights went on momentarily. One of the unit managers left his chair and came and stood in front of Stahr.

"A beautifully acted scene thrown away," raged Stahr quietly. "It wasn't centered. The camera was set up so it caught the beautiful top of Claudette's head all the time she was talking. That's just what we want, isn't it? That's just what people go to see—the top of a beautiful girl's head. Tell Tim he could have saved wear and tear by using her stand-in."

The lights went out again. The unit manager squatted by Stahr's chair to be out of the way. The take was run again.

"Do you see now?" asked Stahr. "And there's a hair in the picture—there on the right, see it? Find out if it's in the projector or the film."

At the very end of the take, Claudette Colbert slowly lifted her head, revealing her great liquid eyes.

"That's what we should have had all the way," said Stahr. "She gave a fine performance too. See if you can fit it in tomorrow or late this afternoon."

Pete Zavras would not have made a slip like that. There were not six camera men in the industry you could entirely trust.

The lights went on; the supervisor and unit manager for that picture went out.

"Monroe, this stuff was shot yesterday—it came through late last night."

The room darkened. On the screen appeared the head of Siva, immense and imperturbable, oblivious to the fact that in a few hours it was to be washed away in a flood. Around it milled a crowd of the faithful.

"When you take that scene again," said Stahr suddenly, "put a couple of little kids up on top. You better check about whether it's reverent or not, but I think it's all right. Kids'll do anything."

"Yes, Monroe."

A silver belt with stars cut out of it. . . . Smith, Jones or Brown. . . . Personal—will the woman with the silver belt who——?

With another picture the scene shifted to New York, a gangster story, and suddenly Stahr became restive.

"That scene's trash," he called suddenly in the darkness. "It's badly written, it's miscast, it accomplishes nothing. Those types aren't tough. They look like a lot of dressed up lollipops—what the hell is the matter, Lee?"

"The scene was written on the set this morning," said Lee Kapper. "Burton wanted to get all the stuff on Stage 6."

"Well—it's trash. And so is this one. There's no use printing stuff like that. She doesn't believe what she's saying—neither does Cary. 'I love you' in a close up—they'll cluck you out of the house! And the girl's overdressed."

In the darkness a signal was given, the projector stopped, the lights went on. The room waited in utter silence. Stahr's face was expressionless.

"Who wrote the scene?" he asked after a minute.

"Wylie White."

"Is he sober?"

"Sure he is."

Stahr considered.

"Put about four writers on that scene tonight," he said. "See who we've got. Is Sidney Howard here yet?"

"He got in this morning."

"Talk to him about it. Explain to him what I want there. The girl is in deadly terror—she's stalling. It's as simple as that. People don't have three emotions at once. And Kapper——"

The art director leaned forward out of the second row.

"Yeah."

"There's something the matter with that set."

There were little glances exchanged all over the room.

"What is it, Monroe?"

"You tell *me*," said Stahr. "It's crowded. It doesn't carry your eye out. It looks cheap."

"It wasn't."

"I know it wasn't. There's not much the matter, but there's something. Go over and take a look tonight. It may be too much furniture—or the wrong kind. Perhaps a window would help. Couldn't you force the perspective in that hall a little more?"

"I'll see what I can do." Kapper edged his way out of the row, looking at his watch.

"I'll have to get at it right away," he said. "I'll work tonight and we'll put it up in the morning."

"All right. Lee, you can shoot around those scenes, can't you?"

"I think so, Monroe."

"I take the blame for this. Have you got the fight stuff?"

"Coming up now."

Stahr nodded. Kapper hurried out, and the room went dark again. On the screen four men staged a terrific socking match in a cellar. Stahr laughed.

"Look at Tracy," he said. "Look at him go down after that guy. I bet he's been in a few."

The men fought over and over. Always the same fight. Always at the end they faced each other smiling, sometimes touching the opponent in a friendly gesture on the shoulder. The only one in danger was the stunt man, a pug who could have murdered the other three. He was in danger only if they swung wild and didn't follow the blows he had taught them. Even so, the youngest actor was afraid for his face and the director had covered his flinches with ingenious angles and interpositions.

And then two men met endlessly in a door, recognized each other and went on. They met, they started, they went on.

Then a little girl read underneath a tree with a boy reading on a limb of the tree above. The little girl was bored and wanted to talk to the boy. He would pay no attention. The core of the apple he was eating fell on the little girl's head.

A voice spoke up out of the darkness:

"It's pretty long, isn't it, Monroe?"

"Not a bit," said Stahr. "It's nice. It has nice feeling."

"I just thought it was long."

"Sometimes ten feet can be too long—sometimes a scene two hundred feet long can be too short. I want to speak to the cutter before he touches this scene—this is something that'll be remembered in the picture."

The oracle had spoken. There was nothing to question or argue. Stahr must be right always, not most of the time, but always—or the structure would melt down like gradual butter.

Another hour passed. Dreams hung in fragments at the far end of the room, suffered analysis, passed—to be dreamed in crowds, or else discarded. The end was signalled by two tests, a character man and a girl. After the rushes, which had a tense rhythm of their own, the tests were smooth and finished; the observers settled in their chairs; Stahr's foot slipped to the floor. Opinions were welcome. One of the technical men let it be known that he would willingly cohabit with the girl; the rest were indifferent.

"Somebody sent up a test of that girl two years ago. She must be getting around—but she isn't getting any better. But the man's good. Can't we use him as the old Russian Prince in *Steppes*?"

"He *is* an old Russian Prince," said the casting director, "but he's ashamed of it. He's a Red. And that's one part he says he wouldn't play."

"It's the only part he could play," said Stahr.

The lights went on. Stahr rolled his gum into its wrapper and put it in an ash-tray. He turned questioningly to his secretary.

"The processes on Stage 2," she said.

He looked in briefly at the processes, moving pictures taken against a background of other moving pictures by an ingenious device. There was a meeting in Marcus' office on the subject of *Manon* with a happy ending, and Stahr had his say on that as he had had before—it had been making money without a happy ending for a century and a half. He was obdurate—at this time in the afternoon he was at his most fluent and the opposition faded into another subject: they would lend a dozen stars to the benefit for those the quake had made homeless at Long Beach. In a sudden burst of giving, five of them all at once made up a purse of twenty-five thousand dollars. They gave well, but not as poor men give. It was not charity.

At his office there was word from the oculist to whom he had sent Pete Zavras that the camera man's eyes were 19-20: approximately perfect. He had written a letter that Zavras was having photostated. Stahr walked around his office cockily while Miss Doolan admired him. Prince Agge had dropped in to thank him for his afternoon on the sets, and while they talked, a cryptic word came from a supervisor that some writers named Tarleton had "found out" and were about to quit.

"These are good writers," Stahr explained to Prince Agge, "and we don't have good writers out here."

"Why, you can hire anyone!" exclaimed his visitor in surprise.

"Oh, we hire them, but when they get out here, they're not good writers—so we have to work with the material we have."

"Such as what?"

"Anybody that'll accept the system and stay decently sober—we have all sorts of people—disappointed poets, one-hit playwrights—college girls—we put them on an idea in pairs, and if it slows down, we put two more writers working behind them. I've had as many as three pairs working independently on the same idea."

"Do they like that?"

"Not if they know about it. They're not geniuses—none of them could make as much any other way. But these Tarletons are a husband and wife team from the East—pretty good playwrights. They've just found out they're not alone on the story and it shocks them—shocks their sense of unity—that's the word they'll use."

"But what does make the—the unity?"

Stahr hesitated—his face was grim except that his eyes twinkled.

"I'm the unity," he said. "Come and see us again."

He saw the Tarletons. He told them he liked their work, looking at Mrs. Tarleton as if he could read her handwriting through the typescript. He told them kindly that he was taking them from the picture and putting them on another, where there was less pressure, more time. As he had half expected, they begged to stay on the first picture, seeing a quicker credit, even though it was shared with others. The system was a shame, he admitted—gross, commercial, to be deplored. He had originated it—a fact that he did not mention.

When they had gone, Miss Doolan came in triumphant.

"Mr. Stahr, the lady with the belt is on the phone."

Stahr walked into his office alone and sat down behind his desk and picked up the phone with a great sinking of his stomach. He did not know what he wanted. He had not thought about the matter as he had thought about the matter of Pete Zavras. At first he had only wanted to know if they were "professional" people, if the woman was an actress who had got herself up to look like Minna, as he had once had a young actress made up like Claudette Colbert and photographed her from the same angles.

"Hello," he said.

"Hello."

As he searched the short, rather surprised word for a vibration of last night, the feeling of terror began to steal over him, and he choked it off with an effort of will.

"Well—you were hard to find," he said. "*Smith*—and you moved here recently. That was all we had. And a silver belt."

"Oh, yes," the voice said, still uneasy, unpoised, "I had on a silver belt last night."

Now, where from here?

"Who *are* you?" the voice said, with a touch of flurried bourgeois dignity.

"My name is Monroe Stahr," he said.

A pause. It was a name that never appeared on the screen, and she seemed to have trouble placing it.

"Oh, yes—yes. You were the husband of Minna Davis."

"Yes."

Was it a trick? As the whole vision of last night came back to him—the very skin with that peculiar radiance as if phosphorus had touched it—he thought whether it might not be a trick to reach him from somewhere. Not Minna and yet Minna. The curtains blew suddenly into the room, the papers whispered on his desk, and his heart cringed faintly at the intense reality of the day outside his window. If he could go out now this way, what would happen if he saw her again—the starry veiled expression, the mouth strongly formed for poor brave human laughter.

"I'd like to see you. Would you like to come to the studio?"

Again the hesitancy—then a blank refusal.

"Oh, I don't think I ought to. I'm awfully sorry."

This last was purely formal, a brush-off, a final axe. Ordinary skin-deep vanity came to Stahr's aid, adding persuasion to his urgency.

"I'd like to see you," he said. "There's a reason."

"Well—I'm afraid that——"

"Could I come and see you?"

A pause again, not from hesitation, he felt, but to assemble her answer.

"There's something you don't know," she said finally.

"Oh, you're probably married," he was impatient. "It has nothing to do with that. I asked you to come here openly, bring your husband if you have one."

"It's—it's quite impossible."

"Why?"

"I feel silly even talking to you, but your secretary insisted—I thought I'd dropped something in the flood last night and you'd found it."

"I want very much to see you for five minutes."

"To put me in the movies?"

"That wasn't my idea."

There was such a long pause that he thought he had offended her.

"Where could I meet you?" she asked unexpectedly.

"Here? At your house?"

"No—somewhere outside."

Suddenly Stahr could think of no place. His own house—a restaurant? Where did people meet?—a house of assignation, a cocktail bar?

"I'll meet you somewhere at nine o'clock," she said.

"That's impossible, I'm afraid."

"Then never mind."

"All right, then, nine o'clock, but can we make it near here? There's a drug-store on Wilshire——"

It was a quarter to six. There were two men outside who had come every day at this time only to be postponed. This was an hour of fatigue—the men's business was not so important that it must be seen to, nor so insignificant that it could be ignored. So he postponed it again and sat motionless at his desk for a moment, thinking about Russia. Not so much about Russia as about the picture about Russia which would consume a hopeless half hour presently. He knew there were many stories about Russia, not to mention The Story, and he had employed a squad of writers and research men for over a year, but all the stories involved had the wrong feel. He felt it could be told in terms of the American thirteen states, but it kept coming out different, in new terms that opened unpleasant possibilities and problems. He considered he was very fair to Russia—he had no desire to make anything but a sympathetic picture, but it kept turning into a headache.

"Mr. Stahr—Mr. Drummon's outside, and Mr. Kirstoff and Mrs. Cornhill, about the Russian picture."

"All right—send them in."

Afterwards from six-thirty to seven-thirty he watched the afternoon rushes. Except for his engagement with the girl, he would ordinarily have spent the early evening in the projection room or the dubbing room, but it had been a late night with the earthquake, and he decided to go to dinner. Coming in through his front office, he found Pete Zavras waiting, his arm in a sling.

"You are the Aeschylus and the Euripides of the moving picture," said Zavras simply. "Also the Aristophanes and the Menander."

He bowed.

"Who are they?" asked Stahr smiling.

"They are my countrymen."

"I didn't know you made pictures in Greece."

"You're joking with me, Monroe," said Zavras. "I want to say you are as dandy a fellow as they come. You have saved me one hundred percent."

"You feel all right now?"

"My arm is nothing. It feels like someone kisses me there. It was worth doing what I did, if this is the outcome."

"How did you happen to do it here?" Stahr asked curiously.

"Before the Delphic oracle," said Zavras. "The Oedipus who solved the riddle. I wish I had my hands on the son-of-a-bitch who started the story."

"You make me sorry I didn't get an education," said Stahr.

"It isn't worth a damn," said Pete. "I took my baccalaureate in Salonika and look how I ended up."

"Not quite," said Stahr.

"If you want anybody's throat cut anytime day or night," said Zavras, "my number is in the book."

Stahr closed his eyes and opened them again. Zavras' silhouette had blurred a little against the sun. He hung on to the table behind him and said in an ordinary voice.

"Good luck, Pete."

The room was almost black, but he made his feet move, following a pattern, into his office and waited till the door clicked shut before he felt for the pills. The water decanter clattered against the table; the glass clacked. He sat down in a big chair, waiting for the benzedrine to take effect before he went to dinner.

As Stahr walked back from the commissary, a hand waved at him from an open roadster. From the heads showing over the back he recognized a young actor and his girl, and watched them disappear through the gate, already part of the summer twilight. Little by little he was losing the feel of such things, until it seemed that Minna had taken their poignancy with her; his apprehension of splendor was fading so that presently the luxury of eternal mourning would depart. A childish association of Minna with the material heavens made him, when he reached his office, order out his roadster for the first time this year. The big limousine seemed heavy with remembered conferences or exhausted sleep.

Leaving the studio, he was still tense, but the open car pulled the summer evening up close, and he looked at it. There was a moon down at the end of the boulevard, and it was a good illusion that it was a different moon every evening, every year. Other lights shone in Hollywood since Minna's death: in the open markets lemons and grapefruit and green apples slanted a misty glare into the street. Ahead of him the stop-signal of a car winked violet and at another crossing he watched it wink again. Everywhere floodlights raked the sky. On an empty corner two mysterious men moved a gleaming drum in pointless arcs over the heavens.

In the drug-store a woman stood by the candy counter. She was tall, almost as tall as Stahr, and embarrassed. Obviously it was a situation for her, and if Stahr had not looked as he did—most considerate and polite—she would not have gone through with it. They said hello, and walked out without another word, scarcely a glance —yet before they reached the curb Stahr knew: this was just exactly a pretty American woman and nothing more—no beauty like Minna.

"Where are we going?" she asked. "I thought there'd be a chauffeur. Never mind—I'm a good boxer."

"Boxer?"

"That didn't sound very polite." She forced a smile. "But you people are supposed to be such *horrors*."

The conception of himself as sinister amused Stahr—then suddenly it failed to amuse him.

"Why did you want to see me?" she asked as she got in.

He stood motionless, wanting to tell her to get out immediately. But she had relaxed in the car, and he knew the unfortunate situation was of his own making—he shut his teeth and walked around to get in. The street lamp fell full upon her face, and it was difficult to believe that this was the girl of last night. He saw no resemblance to Minna at all.

"I'll run you home," he said. "Where do you live?"

"Run me home?" She was startled. "There's no hurry—I'm sorry if I offended you."

"No. It was nice of you to come. I've been stupid. Last night I had an idea that you were an exact double for someone I knew. It was dark and the light was in my eyes."

She was offended—he had reproached her for not looking like someone else.

"It was just that!" she said. "That's funny."

They rode in silence for a minute.

"You were married to Minna Davis, weren't you?" she said with a flash of intuition. "Excuse me for referring to it."

He was driving as fast as he could without making it conspicuous.

"I'm quite a different type from Minna Davis," she said, "—if that's who you meant. You might have referred to the girl who was with me. She looks more like Minna Davis than I do."

That was of no interest now. The thing was to get this over quick and forget it.

"Could it have been her?" she asked. "She lives next door."

"Not possibly," he said. "I remember the silver belt you wore."

"That was me all right."

They were northwest of Sunset, climbing one of the canyons through the hills. Lighted bungalows rose along the winding road, and the electric current that animated them sweated into the evening air as radio sound.

"You see that last highest light—Kathleen lives there. I live just over the top of the hill."

A moment later she said, "Stop here."

"I thought you said over the top."

"I want to stop at Kathleen's."

"I'm afraid I'm——"

"I want to get out here myself," she said impatiently.

Stahr slid out after her. She started toward a new little house almost roofed over by a single willow tree, and automatically he followed her to the steps. She rang a bell and turned to say good night.

"I'm sorry you were disappointed," she said.

He was sorry for her now—sorry for them both.

"It was my fault. Good night."

A wedge of light came out the opening door, and as a girl's voice inquired, "Who is it?" Stahr looked up.

There she was—face and form and smile against the light from inside. It was Minna's face—the skin with its peculiar radiance as if phosphorus had touched it, the mouth with its warm line that never counted costs—and over all the haunting jollity that had fascinated a generation.

With a leap his heart went out of him as it had the night before, only this time it stayed out there with a vast beneficence.

"Oh, Edna, you can't come in," the girl said. "I've been cleaning and the house is full of ammonia smell."

Edna began to laugh, bold and loud. "I believe it was you he wanted to see, Kathleen," she said.

Stahr's eyes and Kathleen's met and tangled. For an instant they made love as no one ever dares to do after. Their glance was slower than an embrace, more urgent than a call.

"He telephoned me," said Edna. "It seems he thought——"

Stahr interrupted, stepping forward into the light.

"I was afraid we were rude at the studio, yesterday evening."

But there were no words for what he really said. She listened closely without shame. Life flared high in them both—Edna seemed at a distance and in darkness.

"You weren't rude," said Kathleen. A cool wind blew the brown curls around her forehead. "We had no business there."

"I hope you'll both," Stahr said, "come and make a tour of the studio."

"Who are you? Somebody important?"

"He was Minna Davis's husband, he's a producer," said Edna,

as if it were a rare joke, "—and this isn't at all what he just told me. I think he has a crush on you."

"Shut up, Edna," said Kathleen sharply.

As if suddenly realizing her offensiveness, Edna said, "Phone me, will you?" and stalked away toward the road. But she carried their secret with her—she had seen a spark pass between them in the darkness.

"I remember you," Kathleen said to Stahr. "You got us out of the flood."

Now what? The other woman was more missed in her absence. They were alone and on too slim a basis for what had passed already. They existed nowhere. His world seemed far away—she had no world at all except the idol's head, the half open door.

"You're Irish," he said, trying to build one for her.

She nodded.

"I've lived in London a long time—I didn't think you could tell."

The wild green eyes of a bus sped up the road in the darkness. They were silent until it went by.

"Your friend Edna didn't like me," he said. "I think it was the word Producer."

"She's just come out here, too. She's a silly creature who means no harm. *I* shouldn't be afraid of you."

She searched his face. She thought, like everyone, that he seemed tired—then she forgot it at the impression he gave of a brazier out of doors on a cool night.

"I suppose the girls are all after you to put them on the screen."

"They've given up," he said.

This was an understatement—they were all there, he knew, just over his threshold, but they had been there so long that their clamoring voices were no more than the sound of the traffic in the street. But his position remained more than royal: a king could make only one queen; Stahr, at least so they supposed, could make many.

"I'm thinking that it would turn you into a cynic," she said. "You didn't want to put me in the pictures?"

"No."

"That's good. I'm no actress. Once in London a man came up to me in the Carlton and asked me to make a test, but I thought awhile and finally I didn't go."

They had been standing nearly motionless, as if in a moment he would leave and she would go in. Stahr laughed suddenly.

"I feel as if I had my foot in the door—like a collector."

She laughed, too.

"I'm sorry I can't ask you in. Shall I get my reefer and sit outside?"

"No." He scarcely knew why he felt it was time to go. He might see her again—he might not. It was just as well this way.

"You'll come to the studio?" he said. "I can't promise to go around with you, but if you come, you must be sure to send word to my office."

A frown, the shadow of a hair in breadth, appeared between her eyes.

"I'm not sure," she said. "But I'm very much obliged."

He knew that, for some reason, she would not come—in an instant she had slipped away from him. They both sensed that the moment was played out. He must go, even though he went nowhere, and it left him with nothing. Practically, vulgarly, he did not have her telephone number—or even her name; but it seemed impossible to ask for them now.

She walked with him to the car, her glowing beauty and her unexplored novelty pressing up against him; but there was a foot of moonlight between them when they came out of the shadow.

"Is this all?" he said spontaneously.

He saw regret in her face—but there was a flick of the lip, also, a bending of the smile toward some indirection, a momentary dropping and lifting of a curtain over a forbidden passage.

"I do hope we'll meet again," she said almost formally.

"I'd be sorry if we didn't."

They were distant for a moment. But as he turned his car in the next drive and came back with her still waiting, and waved and drove on, he felt exalted and happy. He was glad that there was beauty in the world that would not be weighed in the scales of the casting department.

But at home he felt a curious loneliness as his butler made him tea in the samovar. It was the old hurt come back, heavy and delightful. When he took up the first of two scripts that were his evening stint, that presently he would visualize line by line on the screen, he waited a moment, thinking of Minna. He explained to her that it was really nothing, that no one could ever be like she was, that he was sorry.

That was substantially a day of Stahr's. I don't know about the illness, when it started, etc., because he was secretive, but I know he fainted a couple of times that month because Father told me. Prince Agge is my authority for the luncheon in the commissary where he told them he was going to make a picture that would lose money —which was something, considering the men he had to deal with and that he held a big block of stock and had a profit-sharing contract.

And Wylie White told me a lot, which I believed because he felt Stahr intensely with a mixture of jealousy and admiration. As for me, I was head over heels in love with him then, and you can take what I say for what it's worth.

CHAPTER V

FRESH AS the morning, I went up to see him a week later. Or so I thought; when Wylie called for me, I had gotten into riding clothes to give the impression I'd been out in the dew since early morning.

"I'm going to throw myself under the wheel of Stahr's car, this morning," I said.

"How about this car?" he suggested. "It's one of the best cars Mort Fleishacker ever sold second-hand."

"Not on your flowing veil," I answered like a book. "You have a wife in the East."

"She's the past," he said. "You've got one great card, Celia—your valuation of yourself. Do you think anybody would look at you if you weren't Pat Brady's daughter?"

We don't take abuse like our mothers would have. Nothing—no remark from a contemporary means much. They tell you to be smart, they're marrying you for your money, or you tell them. Everything's simpler. Or is it? as we used to say.

But as I turned on the radio and the car raced up Laurel Canyon to *The Thundering Beat of My Heart,* I didn't believe he was right. I had good features except my face was too round, and a skin they seemed to love to touch, and good legs, and I didn't have to wear a brassiere. I haven't a sweet nature, but who was Wylie to reproach me for that?

"Don't you think I'm smart to go in the morning?" I asked.

"Yeah. To the busiest man in California. He'll appreciate it. Why didn't you wake him up at four?"

"That's just it. At night he's tired. He's been looking at people all day, and some of them not bad. I come in in the morning and start a train of thought."

"I don't like it. It's brazen."

"What have you got to offer? And don't be rough."

68

"I love you," he said, without much conviction, "I love you more than I love your money, and that's plenty. Maybe your father would make me a supervisor."

"I could marry the last man tapped for Bones this year and live in Southampton."

I turned the dial and got either *Gone* or *Lost*—there were good songs that year. The music was getting better again. When I was young during the depression, it wasn't so hot, and the bes* numbers were from the twenties, like Benny Goodman playing *Blue Heaven* or Paul Whiteman with *When Day Is Done*. There were only the bands to listen to. But now I liked almost everything except Father singing *Little Girl, You've Had a Busy Day* to try to create a senti-mental father-and-daughter feeling.

Lost and *Gone* were the wrong mood, so I turned again and got *Lovely to Look At*, which was my kind of poetry. I looked back as we crossed the crest of the foothills—with the air so clear you could see the leaves on Sunset Mountain two miles away. It's startling to you sometimes—just air, unobstructed, uncomplicated air.

"*Lovely to look at—de-lightful to know-w,*" I sang.

"Are you going to sing for Stahr?" Wylie said. "If you do, get in a line about my being a good supervisor."

"Oh, this'll be only Stahr and me," I said. "He's going to look at me and think, 'I've never really seen her before.'"

"We don't use that line this year," he said.

"—Then he'll say 'Little Cecilia,' like he did the night of the earthquake. He'll say he never noticed I have become a woman."

"You won't have to do a thing."

"I'll stand there and bloom. After he kisses me as you would a child——"

"That's all in my script," complained Wylie, "and I've got to show it to him tomorrow."

"—he'll sit down and put his face in his hands and say he never thought of me like that."

"You mean you get in a little fast work during the kiss?"

"I bloom, I told you. How often do I have to tell you I bloom."

"It's beginning to sound pretty randy to me," said Wylie. "How about laying off—I've got to work this morning."

"Then he says it seems as if he was always meant to be this way."

"Right in the industry. Producer's blood." He pretended to shiver. "I'd hate to have a transfusion of that."

"Then he says——"

"I know all his lines," said Wylie. "What I want to know is what you say."

"Somebody comes in," I went on.

"And you jump up quickly off the casting couch, smoothing your skirts."

"Do you want me to walk out and get home?"

We were in Beverly Hills, getting very beautiful now with the tall Hawaiian pines. Hollywood is a perfectly zoned city, so you know exactly what kind of people economically live in each section, from executives and directors, through technicians in their bungalows, right down to extras. This was the executive section and a very fancy lot of pastry. It wasn't as romantic as the dingiest village of Virginia or New Hampshire, but it looked nice this morning.

"*They asked me how I knew,*" sang the radio, "*—my true love was true.*"

My heart was fire, and smoke was in my eyes and everything, but I figured my chance at about fifty-fifty. I would walk right up to him as if I was either going to walk through him or kiss him on the mouth—and stop a bare foot away and say "Hello" with disarming understatement.

And I did—though of course it wasn't like I expected: Stahr's beautiful dark eyes looking back into mine, knowing, I am dead sure, everything I was thinking—and not a bit embarrassed. I stood there an hour, I think, without moving, and all he did was twitch the side of his mouth and put his hands in his pocket.

"Will you go with me to the ball tonight?" I asked.

"What ball?"

"The screen-writers' ball down at the Ambassador."

"Oh, yes." He considered. "I can't go with you. I might just come in late. We've got a sneak preview in Glendale."

How different it all was from what you'd planned. When he sat down, I went over and put my head among his telephones, like a sort of desk appendage, and looked at him; and his dark eyes looked back so kind and nothing. Men don't often know those times when a girl could be had for nothing. All I succeeded in putting into his head was:

"Why don't you get married, Celia?"

Maybe he'd bring up Robby again, try to make a match there.

"What could I do to interest an interesting man?" I asked him.

"Tell him you're in love with him."

"Should I chase him?"

"Yes," he said smiling.

"I don't know. If it isn't there, it isn't there."

"I'd marry you," he said unexpectedly. "I'm lonesome as hell. But I'm too old and tired to undertake anything."

I went around the desk and stood beside him.

"Undertake me."

He looked up in surprise, understanding for the first time that I was in deadly earnest.

"Oh, no," he said. He looked almost miserable for a minute. "Pictures are my girl. I haven't got much time——" He corrected himself quickly, "I mean any time. It'd be like marrying a doctor."

"You couldn't love me "

"It's not that," he said and—right out of my dream but with a difference: "I never thought of you that way, Celia. I've known you so long. Somebody told me you were going to marry Wylie White."

"And you had—no reaction."

"Yes, I did. I was going to speak to you about it. Wait till he's been sober for two years."

"I'm not even considering it, Monroe."

We were way off the track, and just as in my day-dream somebody came in—only I was quite sure Stahr had pressed a concealed button.

I'll always think of that moment, when I felt Miss Doolan behind me with her pad, as the end of childhood, the end of the time when you cut out pictures. What I was looking at wasn't Stahr but a picture of him I cut out over and over: the eyes that flashed a sophisticated understanding at you and then darted up too soon into his wide brow with its ten thousand plots and plans; the face that was aging from within, so that there were no casual furrows of worry and vexation but a drawn asceticism·as if from a silent self-set struggle—or a long illness. It was handsomer to me than all the rosy tan from Coronado to Del Monte. He was my picture, as sure as if he had been pasted on the inside of my old locker in school. That's what I told Wylie White, and when a girl tells the man she likes second best about the other one—then she's in love.

I noticed the girl long before Stahr arrived at the dance. Not a pretty girl, for there are none of those in Los Angeles—one girl can be pretty, but a dozen are only a chorus. Nor yet a professional beauty—they do all the breathing for everyone, and finally even the men have to go outside for air. Just a girl, with the skin of one of Raphael's corner angels and a style that made you look back twice to see if it were something she had on.

I noticed her and forgot her. She was sitting back behind the pillars at a table whose ornament was a faded semi-star, who, in hopes of being noticed and getting a bit, rose and danced regularly with some scarecrow males. It reminded me shamefully of my first party, where mother made me dance over and over with the same boy to keep in the spotlight. The semi-star spoke to several people at our table, but we were busy being Café Society and she got nowhere at all.

From our angle it appeared that they all wanted something.

"You're expected to fling it around," said Wylie, "—like in the old days. When they find out you're hanging on to it, they get discouraged. That's what all this brave gloom is about—the only way to keep their self-respect is to be Hemingway characters. But underneath they hate you in a mournful way, and you know it."

He was right—I knew that since 1933 the rich could only be happy alone together.

I saw Stahr come into the half-light at the top of the wide steps and stand there with his hands in his pockets, looking around. It was late and the lights seemed to have burned a little lower, though they were the same. The floor show was finished, except for a man who still wore a placard which said that at midnight in the Hollywood Bowl Sonja Henie was going to skate on hot soup. You could see the sign as he danced becoming less funny on his back. A few years before there would have been drunks around. The faded actress seemed to be looking for them hopefully over her partner's

shoulder. I followed her with my eyes when she went back to her
table——

——and there, to my surprise, was Stahr talking to the other girl.
They were smiling at each other as if this was the beginning of
the world.

Stahr had expected nothing like this when he stood at the head
of the steps a few minutes earlier. The "sneak preview" had disappointed him, and afterwards he had had a scene with Jacques
La Borwitz right in front of the theatre, for which he was now
sorry. He had started toward the Brady party when he saw Kathleen
sitting in the middle of a long white table alone.

Immediately things changed. As he walked toward her, the people
shrank back against the walls till they were only murals; the white
table lengthened and became an altar where the priestess sat alone.
Vitality welled up in him, and he could have stood a long time across
the table from her, looking and smiling.

The incumbents of the table were crawling back—Stahr and
Kathleen danced.

When she came close, his several visions of her blurred; she was
momentarily unreal. Usually a girl's skull made her real, but not this
time—Stahr continued to be dazzled as they danced out along the
floor—to the last edge, where they stepped through a mirror into
another dance with new dancers whose faces were familiar but nothing more. In this new region he talked, fast and urgently.

"What's your name?"

"Kathleen Moore."

"Kathleen Moore," he repeated.

"I have no telephone, if that's what you're thinking."

"When will you come to the studio?"

"It's not possible. Truly."

"Why isn't it? Are you married?"

"No."

"You're not married?"

"No, nor never have been. But then I may be."

"Someone there at the table."

"No." She laughed. "What curiosity!"

But she was deep in it with him, no matter what the words were.

Her eyes invited him to a romantic communion of unbelievable intensity. As if she realized this, she said, frightened:

"I must go back now. I promised this dance."

"I don't want to lose you. Couldn't we have lunch or dinner?"

"It's impossible." But her expression helplessly amended the words to, "It's just possible. The door is still open by a chink, if you could squeeze past. But quickly—so little time."

"I must go back," she repeated aloud. Then she dropped her arms, stopped dancing, and looked at him, a laughing wanton.

"When I'm with you, I don't breathe quite right," she said.

She turned, picked up her long dress, and stepped back through the mirror. Stahr followed until she stopped near her table.

"Thank you for the dance," she said, "and now really, good night."

Then she nearly ran.

Stahr went to the table where he was expected and sat down with the Café Society group—from Wall Street, Grand Street, Loudon County, Virginia, and Odessa, Russia. They were all talking with enthusiasm about a horse that had run very fast, and Mr. Marcus was the most enthusiastic of all. Stahr guessed that the Jews had taken over the worship of horses as a symbol—for years it had been the Cossacks mounted and the Jews on foot. Now the Jews had horses, and it gave them a sense of extraordinary well-being and power. Stahr sat pretending to listen and even nodding when something was referred to him, but all the time watching the table behind the pillars. If everything had not happened as it had, even to his connecting the silver belt with the wrong girl, he might have thought it was some elaborate frame-up. But the elusiveness was beyond suspicion. For there in a moment he saw that she was escaping again—the pantomime at the table indicated goodbye. She was leaving, she was gone.

"There," said Wylie White with malice, "goes Cinderella. Simply bring the slipper to the Regal Shoe Company, 812 South Broadway."

Stahr overtook her in the long upper lobby, where middle-aged women sat behind a roped-off space, watching the ballroom entrance.

"Am I responsible for this?" he asked.

"I was going anyhow." But she added almost resentfully, "They talked as if I'd been dancing with the Prince of Wales. They all stared at me. One of the men wanted to draw my picture, and another one wanted to see me tomorrow."

"That's just what I want," said Stahr gently, "but I want to see you much more than he does."

"You insist so," she said wearily. "One reason I left England was that men always wanted their own way. I thought it was different here. Isn't it enough that I don't want to see you?"

"Ordinarily," agreed Stahr. "Please believe me, I'm way out of my depth already. I feel like a fool. But I must see you again and talk to you."

She hesitated.

"There's no reason for feeling like a fool," she said. "You're too good a man to feel like a fool. But you should see this for what it is."

"What is it?"

"You've fallen for me—completely. You've got me in your dreams."

"I'd forgotten you," he declared, "—till the moment I walked in that door."

"Forgotten me with your head perhaps. But I knew the first time I saw you that you were the kind that likes me——"

She stopped herself. Near them a man and woman from the party were saying goodbye: "Tell her hello—tell her I love her dearly," said the woman, "—you both—all of you—the children." Stahr could not talk like that, the way everyone talked now. He could think of nothing further to say as they walked toward the elevator except: "I suppose you're perfectly right."

"Oh, you admit it?"

"No, I don't," he retracted. "It's just the whole way you're made. What you say—how you walk—the way you look right this minute—" He saw she had melted a little, and his hopes rose. "Tomorrow is Sunday, and usually I work on Sunday, but if there's anything you're curious about in Hollywood, any person you want to meet or see, please let me arrange it."

They were standing by the elevator. It opened, but she let it go. "You're very modest," she said. "You always talk about showing me the studio and taking me around. Don't you ever stay alone?"

"'Tomorrow I'll feel very much alone."

"Oh, the poor man—I could weep for him. He could have all the stars jumping around him and he chooses me."

He smiled—he had laid himself open to that one.

The elevator came again. She signalled for it to wait.

"I'm a weak woman," she said. "If I meet you tomorrow, will you leave me in peace? No, you won't. You'll make it worse. It wouldn't do any good but harm, so I'll say no and thank you."

She got into the elevator. Stahr got in too, and they smiled as they dropped two floors to the hall, cross-sectioned with small shops. Down at the end, held back by police, was the crowd, their heads and shoulders leaning forward to look down the alley. Kathleen shivered.

"They looked so strange when I came in," she said, "—as if they were furious at me for not being someone famous."

"I know another way out," said Stahr.

They went through a drug-store, down an alley, and came out into the clear cool California night beside the car park. He felt detached from the dance now, and she did, too.

"A lot of picture people used to live down here," he said. "John Barrymore and Pola Negri in those bungalows. And Connie Talmadge lived in that tall thin apartment house over the way."

"Doesn't anybody live here now?"

"The studios moved out into the country," he said, "—what used to be the country. I had some good times around here, though."

He did not mention that ten years ago Minna and her mother had lived in another apartment over the way.

"How old are you?" she asked suddenly.

"I've lost track—almost thirty-five, I think."

"They said at the table you were the boy wonder."

"I'll be that when I'm sixty," he said grimly. "You will meet me tomorrow, won't you?"

"I'll meet you," she said. "Where?"

Suddenly there was no place to meet. She would not go to a party at anyone's house, nor to the country, nor swimming, though she hesitated, nor to a well-known restaurant. She seemed hard to please, but he knew there was some reason. He would find out in time. It occurred to him that she might be the sister or daughter of someone well-known, who was pledged to keep in the background. He suggested that he come for her and they could decide.

"That wouldn't do," she said. "What about right here?—the same spot."

He nodded—pointing up at the arch under which they stood.

He put her into her car, which would have brought eighty dollars from any kindly dealer, and watched it rasp away. Down by the entrance a cheer went up as a favorite emerged, and Stahr wondered whether to show himself and say good night.

This is Cecilia taking up the narrative in person. Stahr came back finally—it was about half past three—and asked me to dance.

"How are you?" he asked me, just as if he hadn't seen me that morning. "I got involved in a long conversation with a man."

It was secret, too—he cared that much about it.

"I took him for a drive," he went on innocently. "I didn't realize how much this part of Hollywood had changed."

"Has it changed?"

"Oh, yes," he said, "—changed completely. Unrecognizable. I couldn't tell you exactly, but it's all changed—everything. It's like a new city." After a moment he amplified: "I had no idea how much it had changed."

"Who was the man?" I ventured.

"An old friend," he said vaguely, "—someone I knew a long time ago."

I had made Wylie try to find out quietly who she was. He had gone over and the ex-star had asked him excitedly to sit down. No: she didn't know who the girl was—a friend of a friend of someone —even the man who had brought her didn't know.

So Stahr and I danced to the beautiful music of Glenn Miller playing *I'm on a See-Saw*. It was good dancing now, with plenty of room. But it was lonely—lonelier than before the girl had gone. For me, as well as for Stahr, she took the evening with her, took along the stabbing pain I had felt—left the great ballroom empty and without emotion. Now it was nothing, and I was dancing with an absent-minded man who told me how much Los Angeles had changed.

They met, next afternoon, as strangers in an unfamiliar country. Last night was gone, the girl he had danced with was gone. A misty rose-and-blue hat with a trifling veil came along the terrace to him, and paused, searching his face. Stahr was strange, too, in a brown suit and a black tie that blocked him out more tangibly than a formal dinner coat, or when he was simply a face and voice in the darkness the night they had first met.

He was the first to be sure it was the same person as before: the upper half of the face that was Minna's, luminous, with creamy temples and opalescent brow—the cocoa-colored curly hair. He could have put his arm around her and pulled her close with an almost family familiarity—already he knew the down on her neck, the very set of her backbone, the corners of her eyes, and how she breathed—the very texture of the clothes that she would wear.

"Did you wait here all night," she said, in a voice that was like a whisper.

"I didn't move—didn't stir."

Still a problem remained, the same one—there was no special place to go.

"I'd like tea," she suggested, "—if it's some place you're not known."

"That sounds as if one of us had a bad reputation."

"Doesn't it?" she laughed.

"We'll go to the shore," Stahr suggested. "There's a place there where I got out once and was chased by a trained seal."

"Do you think the seal could make tea?"

"Well—he's trained. And I don't think he'll talk—I don't think his training got that far. What in *hell* are you trying to hide?"

After a moment she said lightly: "Perhaps the future," in a way that might mean anything or nothing at all.

As they drove away, she pointed at her jalopy in the parking lot.

"Do you think it's safe?"

"I doubt it. I noticed some black-bearded foreigners snooping around."

Kathleen looked at him alarmed.

"Really?" She saw he was smiling. "I believe everything you say," she said. "You've got such a gentle way about you that I don't see why they're all so afraid of you." She examined him with approval—fretting a little about his pallor, which was accentuated by the bright afternoon. "Do you work very hard? Do you really always work on Sundays?"

He responded to her interest—impersonal yet not perfunctory.

"Not always. Once we had—we had a house with a pool and all—and people came on Sunday. I played tennis and swam. I don't swim any more."

"Why not? It's good for you. I thought all Americans swam."

"My legs got very thin—a few years ago, and it embarrassed me. There were other things I used to do—lots of things: I used to play handball when I was a kid, and sometimes out here—I had a court that was washed away in a storm."

"You have a good build," she said in formal compliment, meaning only that he was made with thin grace.

He rejected this with a shake of his head.

"I enjoy working most," he said. "My work is very congenial."

"Did you always want to be in movies?"

"No. When I was young I wanted to be a chief clerk—the one who knew where everything was."

She smiled.

"That's odd. And now you're much more than that."

"No, I'm still a chief clerk," Stahr said. "That's my gift, if I have one. Only when I got to be it, I found out that no one knew where anything was. And I found out that you had to know why it was where it was, and whether it should be left there. They began throwing it all at me, and it was a very complex office. Pretty soon I had all the keys. And they wouldn't have remembered what locks they fitted if I'd given them back."

They stopped for a red light, and a newsboy bleated at him: "Mickey Mouse Murdered! Randolph Hearst declares war on China!"

"We'll have to buy his paper," she said.

As they drove on, she straightened her hat and preened herself. Seeing him looking at her, she smiled.

She was alert and calm—qualities that were currently at a

premium. There was lassitude in plenty—California was filling up with weary desperadoes. And there were tense young men and women who lived back East in spirit while they carried on a losing battle against the climate. But it was everyone's secret that sustained effort was difficult here—a secret that Stahr scarcely admitted to himself. But he knew that people from other places spurted a pure rill of new energy for awhile.

They were very friendly now. She had not made a move or a gesture that was out of keeping with her beauty, that pressed it out of its contour one way or another. It was all proper to itself. He judged her as he would a shot in 'a picture. She was not trash, she was not confused but clear—in his special meaning of the word, which implied balance, delicacy and proportion, she was "nice."

They reached Santa Monica, where there were the stately houses of a dozen picture stars, penned in the middle of a crawling Coney Island. They turned down hill into the wide blue sky and sea and went on along the sea till the beach slid out again from under the bathers in a widening and narrowing yellow strand.

"I'm building a house out here," Stahr said, "—much further on. I don't know why I'm building it."

"Perhaps it's for me," she said.

"Maybe it is."

"I think it's splendid for you to build a big house for me without even knowing what I looked like."

"It isn't so big. And it hasn't any roof. I didn't know what kind of roof you wanted."

"We don't want a roof. They told me it never rained here. It—"

She stopped so suddenly that he knew she was reminded of something.

"Just something that's past," she said.

"What was it?" he demanded, "—another house without a roof?"

"Yes. Another house without a roof."

"Were you happy there?"

"I lived with a man," she said, "a long, long time—too long. It was one of those awful mistakes people make. I lived with him a long time after I wanted to get out, but he couldn't let me go. He'd try, but he couldn't. So finally I ran away."

He was listening, weighing but not judging. Nothing changed

under the rose and blue hat. She was twenty-five or so. It would have been a waste if she had not loved and been loved.

"We were too close," she said. "We should probably have had children—to stand between us. But you can't have children when there's no roof to the house."

All right, he knew something of her. It would not be like last night when something kept saying, as in a story conference: "We know nothing about the girl. We don't have to know much—but we have to know something." A vague background spread behind her, something more tangible than the head of Siva in the moonlight.

They came to the restaurant, forbidding with many Sunday automobiles. When they got out, the trained seal growled reminiscently at Stahr. The man who owned it said that the seal would never ride in the back seat of his car but always climbed over the back and up in front. It was plain that the man was in bondage to the seal, though he had not yet acknowledged it to himself.

"I'd like to see the house you're building," said Kathleen. "I don't want tea—tea is the past."

Kathleen drank a coke instead and they drove on ten miles into a sun so bright that he took out two pairs of cheaters from a compartment. Five miles further on they turned down a small promontory and came to the fuselage of Stahr's house.

A headwind blowing out of the sun threw spray up the rocks and over the car. Concrete mixer, raw yellow wood and builders' rubble waited, an open wound in the seascape, for Sunday to be over. They walked around front, where great boulders rose to what would be the terrace.

She looked at the feeble hills behind and winced faintly at the barren glitter, and Stahr saw—

"No use looking for what's not here," he said cheerfully. "Think of it as if you were standing on one of those globes with a map on it—I always wanted one when I was a boy."

"I understand," she said after a minute. "When you do that, you can feel the earth turn, can't you?"

He nodded.

"Yes. Otherwise it's all just *mañana*—waiting for the morning or the moon."

They went in under the scaffolding. One room, which was to be the chief salon, was completed even to the built-in book shelves and the curtain rods and the trap in the floor for the motion picture projection machine. And to her surprise, this opened out to a porch with cushioned chairs in place and a ping-pong table. There was another ping-pong table on the newly laid sod beyond.

"Last week I gave a premature luncheon," he admitted. "I had some props brought out—some grass and things. I wanted to see how the place felt."

She laughed suddenly.

"Isn't that real grass?"

"Oh, yes—it's grass."

Beyond the strip of anticipatory lawn was the excavation for a swimming pool, patronized now by a crowd of seagulls, which saw them and took flight.

"Are you going to live here all alone?" she asked him, "—not even dancing girls?"

"Probably. I used to make plans, but not any more. I thought this would be a nice place to read scripts. The studio is really home."

"That's what I've heard about American business men."

He caught a tilt of criticism in her voice.

"You do what you're born to do," he said gently. "About once a month somebody tries to reform me, tells me what a barren old age I'll have when I can't work any more. But it's not so simple."

The wind was rising. It was time to go, and he had his car keys out of his pocket, absent-mindedly jingling them in his hand. There was the silvery "hey!" of a telephone, coming from somewhere across the sunshine.

It was not from the house, and they hurried here and there around the garden, like children playing warmer and colder—closing in finally on a tool shack by the tennis court. The phone, irked with delay, barked at them suspiciously from the wall. Stahr hesitated.

"Shall I let the damn thing ring?"

"I couldn't. Unless I was sure who it was."

"Either it's for somebody else or they've made a wild guess."

He picked up the receiver.

"Hello . . . Long distance from where? Yes, this is Mr. Stahr."

His manner changed perceptibly. She saw what few people had

seen for a decade: Stahr impressed. It was not discordant, because he often pretended to be impressed, but it made him momentarily a little younger.

"It's the President," he said to her, almost stiffly.

"Of your company?"

"No, of the United States."

He was trying to be casual for her benefit, but his voice was eager. "All right, I'll wait," he said into the phone, and then to Kathleen: "I've talked to him before."

She watched. He smiled at her and winked, as an evidence that while he must give this his best attention, he had not forgotten her.

"Hello," he said presently. He listened. Then he said, "Hello" again. He frowned.

"Can you talk a little louder," he said politely, and then: "Who? . . . What's that?"

She saw a disgusted look come into his face.

"I don't want to talk to him," he said. "No!"

He turned to Kathleen:

"Believe it or not, it's an orang-outang."

He waited while something was explained to him at length; then he repeated:

"I don't want to talk to it, Lew. I haven't got anything to say that would interest an orang-outang."

He beckoned to Kathleen, and when she came close to the phone, he held the receiver so that she heard odd breathing and a gruff growl. Then a voice:

"This is no phoney, Monroe. It can talk and it's a dead ringer for McKinley. Mr. Horace Wickersham is with me here with a picture of McKinley in his hand——"

Stahr listened patiently.

"We've got a chimp," he said, after a minute. "He bit a chunk out of John Gilbert last year. . . . All right, put him on again."

He spoke formally as if to a child.

"Hello, orang-outang."

His face changed, and he turned to Kathleen.

"He said 'Hello.'"

"Ask him his name," suggested Kathleen.

"Hello, orang-outang—God, what a thing to be!—Do you know

your name? . . . He doesn't seem to know his name. . . . Listen, Lew. We're not making anything like *King Kong,* and there is no monkey in *The Hairy Ape.* . . . Of course I'm sure. I'm sorry, Lew, goodbye."

He was annoyed with Lew because he had thought it was the President and had changed his manner, acting as if it were. He felt a little ridiculous, but Kathleen felt sorry and liked him better because it had been an orang-outang.

They started back along the shore with the sun behind them. The house seemed kindlier when they left it, as if warmed by their visit—the hard glitter of the place was more endurable if they were not bound there like people on the shiny surface of a moon. Looking back from a curve of the shore, they saw the sky growing pink behind the indecisive structure, and the point of land seemed a friendly island, not without promise of fine hours on a further day.

Past Malibu with its gaudy shacks and fishing barges they came into the range of human kind again, the cars stacked and piled along the road, the beaches like ant hills without a pattern, save for the dark drowned heads that sprinkled the sea.

Goods from the city were increasing in sight—blankets, matting, umbrellas, cookstoves, reticules full of clothing—the prisoners had laid out their shackles beside them on this sand. It was Stahr's sea if he wanted it, or knew what to do with it—only by sufferance did these others wet their feet and fingers in the wild cool reservoirs of man's world.

Stahr turned off the road by the sea and up a canyon and along a hill road, and the people dropped away. The hill became the outskirts of the city. Stopping for gasoline, he stood beside the car.

"We could have dinner," he said almost anxiously.

"You have work you could do."

"No—I haven't planned anything. Couldn't we have dinner?"

He knew that she had nothing to do either—no planned evening or special place to go.

She compromised.

"Do you want to get something in that drug-store across the street?"

He looked at it tentatively.

"Is that really what you want?"

"I like to eat in American drug-stores. It seems so queer and strange."

They sat on high stools and had tomato broth and hot sandwiches. It was more intimate than anything they had done, and they both felt a dangerous sort of loneliness, and felt it in each other. They shared in varied scents of the drug-store, bitter and sweet and sour, and the mystery of the waitress, with only the outer part of her hair dyed and black beneath, and, when it was over, the still life of their empty plates—a sliver of potato, a sliced pickle and an olive stone. It was dusk in the street, it seemed nothing to smile at him now when they got into the car.

"Thank you so much. It's been a nice afternoon."

It was not far from her house. They felt the beginning of the hill, and the louder sound of the car in second was the beginning of the end. Lights were on in the climbing bungalows—he turned on the headlights of the car. Stahr felt heavy in the pit of his stomach.

"We'll go out again."

"No," she said quickly, as if she had been expecting this. "I'll write you a letter. I'm sorry I've been so mysterious—it was really a compliment because I like you so much. You should try not to work so hard. You ought to marry again."

"Oh, that isn't what you should say," he broke out protestingly. "This has been you and me today. It may have meant nothing to you—it meant a lot to me. I'd like time to tell you about it."

But if he were to take time it must be in her house, for they were there and she was shaking her head as the car drew up to the door.

"I must go now. I do have an engagement. I didn't tell you."

"That's not true. But it's all right."

He walked to the door with her and stood in his own footsteps of that other night, while she felt in her bag for the key.

"Have you got it?"

"I've got it," she said.

That was the moment to go in, but she wanted to see him once more and she leaned her head to the left, then to the right, trying to catch his face against the last twilight. She leaned too far and too long, and it was natural when his hand touched the back of her upper arm and shoulder and pressed her forward into the darkness of his throat. She shut her eyes, feeling the bevel of the key in her tight-clutched hand. She said "Oh" in an expiring sigh, and then "Oh" again, as he pulled her in close and his chin pushed her cheek around gently. They were both smiling just faintly, and she was frowning, too, as the inch between them melted into darkness.

When they were apart, she shook her head still, but more in wonder than in denial. It came like this then, it was your own fault, now far back, when was the moment? It came like this, and every instant the burden of tearing herself away from them together, from it, was heavier and more unimaginable. He was exultant; she resented and could not blame him, but she would not be part of his exultation, for it was a defeat. So far it was a defeat. And then she thought that if she stopped it being a defeat, broke off and went inside, it was still not a victory. Then it was just nothing.

"This was not my idea," she said, "not at all my idea."

"Can I come in?"

"Oh, no—no."

"Then let's jump in the car and drive somewhere."

With relief, she caught at the exact phrasing—to get away from here immediately, that was accomplishment or sounded like it— as if she were fleeing from the spot of a crime. Then they were in the car, going down hill with the breeze cool in their faces, and she came slowly to herself. Now it was all clear in black and white.

"We'll go back to your house on the beach," she said.

"Back there?"

"Yes—we'll go back to your house. Don't let's talk. I just want to ride."

When they got to the coast again the sky was grey, and at Santa Monica a sudden gust of rain bounced over them. Stahr halted beside the road, put on a raincoat, and lifted the canvas top. "We've got a roof," he said.

The windshield wiper ticked domestically as a grandfather's clock. Sullen cars were leaving the wet beaches and starting back into the city. Further on they ran into fog—the road lost its boundaries on either side, and the lights of cars coming toward them were stationary until just before they flared past.

They had left a part of themselves behind, and they felt light and free in the car. Fog fizzed in at a chink, and Kathleen took off the rose-and-blue hat in a calm, slow way that made him watch tensely, and put it under a strip of canvas in the back seat. She shook out her hair and, when she saw that Stahr was looking at her, she smiled.

The trained seal's restaurant was only a sheen of light off toward the ocean. Stahr cranked down a window and looked for landmarks, but after a few more miles the fog fell away, and just ahead of them the road turned off that led to his house. Out here a moon showed behind the clouds. There was still a shifting light over the sea.

The house had dissolved a little back into its elements. They found the dripping beams of a doorway and groped over mysterious waist-high obstacles to the single finished room, odorous of sawdust and wet wood. When he took her in his arms, they could just see each other's eyes in the half darkness. Presently his rain coat dropped to the floor.

"Wait," she said.

She needed a minute. She did not see how any good could come from this, and though this did not prevent her from being happy and desirous, she needed a minute to think how it was, to go back an hour and know how it had happened. She waited in his arms, moving her head a little from side to side as she had before, only more slowly, and never taking her eyes from his. Then she discovered that he was trembling.

He discovered it at the same time, and his arms relaxed. Immediately she spoke to him coarsely and provocatively, and pulled his face down to hers. Then, with her knees she struggled out of something, still standing up and holding him with one arm, and kicked it off beside the coat. He was not trembling now and he held her again, as they knelt down together and slid to the raincoat on the floor.

Afterwards they lay without speaking, and then he was full of such tender love for her that he held her tight till a stitch tore in her dress. The small sound brought them to reality.

"I'll help you up," he said, taking her hands.

"Not just yet. I was thinking of something."

She lay in the darkness, thinking irrationally that it would be such a bright indefatigable baby, but presently she let him help her up. . . . When she came back into the room, it was lit from a single electric fixture.

"A one-bulb lighting system," he said. "Shall I turn it off?"

"No. It's very nice. I want to see you."

They sat in the wooden frame of the window seat, with the soles of their shoes touching.

"You seem far away," she said.

"So do you."

"Are you surprised?"

"At what?"

"That we're two people again. Don't you always think—hope that you'll be one person, and then find you're still two?"

"I feel very close to you."

"So do I to you," she said.

"Thank you."

"Thank *you*."

They laughed.

"Is this what you wanted?" she asked. "I mean last night."

"Not consciously."

"I wonder when it was settled," she brooded. "There's a moment when you needn't, and then there's another moment when you know nothing in the world could keep it from happening."

This had an experienced ring, and to his surprise he liked her even more. In his mood, which was passionately to repeat yet not recapitulate the past, it was right that it should be that way.

"I *am* rather a trollop," she said, following his thoughts. "I suppose that's why I didn't get on to Edna."

"Who is Edna?"

"The girl you thought was me. The one you phoned to—who lived across the road. She's moved to Santa Barbara."

"You mean she was a tart?"

"So it seems. She went to what you call call-houses."

"That's funny."

"If she had been English, I'd have known right away. But she seemed like everyone else. She only told me just before she went away."

He saw her shiver and got up, putting the raincoat around her shoulders. He opened a closet, and a pile of pillows and beach mattresses fell out on the floor. There was a box of candles, and he lit them around the room, attaching the electric heater where the bulb had been.

"Why was Edna afraid of me?" he asked suddenly.

"Because you were a producer. She had some awful experience or a friend of hers did. Also, I think she was extremely stupid."

"How did you happen to know her?"

"She came over. Maybe she thought I was a fallen sister. She seemed quite pleasant. She said 'Call me Edna' all the time—'Please call me Edna,' so finally I called her Edna and we were friends."

She got off the window seat so he could lay pillows along it and behind her.

"What can I do?" she said. "I'm a parasite."

"No, you're not." He put his arms around her. "Be still. Get warm."

They sat for awhile quiet.

"I know why you liked me at first," she said. "Edna told me."

"What did she tell you?"

"That I looked like—Minna Davis. Several people have told me that."

He leaned away from her and nodded.

"It's here," she said, putting her hands on her cheekbones and distorting her cheeks slightly. "Here and here."

"Yes," said Stahr. "It was very strange. You look more like she actually *looked* than how she was on the screen."

She got up, changing the subject with her gesture as if she were afraid of it.

"I'm warm now," she said. She went to the closet and peered in, came back wearing a little apron with a crystalline pattern like a snowfall. She stared around critically.

"Of course we've just moved in," she said, "—and there's a sort of echo."

She opened the door of the veranda and pulled in two wicker chairs, drying them off. He watched her move, intently, yet half afraid that her body would fail somewhere and break the spell. He had watched women in screen tests and seen their beauty vanish second by second, as if a lovely statue had begun to walk with

the meagre joints of a paper doll. But Kathleen was ruggedly set
on the balls of her feet—the fragility was, as it should be, an
illusion.

"It's stopped raining," she said. "It rained the day I came. Such
an awful rain—so loud—like horses weeing."

He laughed.

"You'll like it. Especially if you've got to stay here. Are you
going to stay here? Can't you tell me now? What's the mystery?"

She shook her head.

"Not now—it's not worth telling."

"Come here then."

She came over and stood near him, and he pressed his cheek
against the cool fabric of the apron.

"You're a tired man," she said, putting her hand in his hair.

"Not that way."

"I didn't mean that way," she said hastily. "I meant you'll work
yourself sick."

"Don't be a mother," he said.

"All right. What shall I be?"

Be a trollop, he thought. He wanted the pattern of his life broken.
If he was going to die soon, like the two doctors said, he wanted to
stop being Stahr for awhile and hunt for love like men who had
no gifts to give, like young nameless men who looked along the
streets in the dark.

"You've taken off my apron," she said gently.

"Yes."

"Would anyone be passing along the beach? Shall we put out the
candles?"

"No, don't put out the candles."

Afterwards she lay half on a white cushion and smiled up at him.

"I feel like Venus on the half shell," she said.

"What made you think of that?"

"Look at me—isn't it Botticelli?"

"I don't know," he said smiling. "It is if you say so."

She yawned.

"I've had such a good time. And I'm very fond of you."

"You know a lot, don't you?"

"What do you mean?"

"Oh, from little things you've said. Or perhaps the way you say them."

She deliberated.

"Not much," she said. "I never went to a university, if that's what you mean. But the man I told you about knew everything and he had a passion for educating me. He made out schedules and made me take courses at the Sorbonne and go to museums. I picked up a little."

"What was he?"

"He was a painter of sorts and a hell-cat. And a lot besides. He wanted me to read Spengler—everything was for that. All the history and philosophy and harmony was all so I could read Spengler, and then I left him before we got to Spengler. At the end I think that was the chief reason he didn't want me to go."

"Who was Spengler?"

"I tell you we didn't get to him," she laughed, "and now I'm forgetting everything very patiently, because it isn't likely I'll ever meet anyone like him again."

"Oh, but you shouldn't forget," said Stahr, shocked. He had an intense respect for learning, a racial memory of the old *schules*. "You shouldn't forget."

"It was just in place of babies."

"You could teach your babies," he said.

"Could I?"

"Sure you could. You could give it to them while they were young. When I want to know anything, I've got to ask some drunken writer. Don't throw it away."

"All right," she said, getting up. "I'll tell it to my children. But it's so endless—the more you know, the more there is just beyond, and it keeps on coming. This man could have been anything if he hadn't been a coward and a fool."

"But you were in love with him."

"Oh, yes—with all my heart." She looked through the window, shading her eyes. "It's light out there. Let's go down to the beach."

He jumped up, exclaiming:

"Why, I think it's the grunion!"

"What?"

"It's tonight. It's in all the papers." He hurried out the door, and she heard him open the door of the car. Presently he returned with a newspaper.

"It's at ten-sixteen. That's five minutes."

"An eclipse or something?"

"Very punctual fish," he said. "Leave your shoes and stockings and come with me."

It was a fine blue night. The tide was at the turn, and the little silver fish rocked off shore waiting for 10.16. A few seconds after the time they came swarming in with the tide, and Stahr and Kathleen stepped over them barefoot as they flicked slip-slop on the sand. A negro man came along the shore toward them, collecting the grunion quickly, like twigs, into two pails. They came in twos and threes and platoons and companies, relentless and exalted and scornful, around the great bare feet of the intruders, as they had come before Sir Francis Drake had nailed his plaque to the boulder on the shore.

"I wish for another pail," the negro man said, resting a moment.

"You've come a long way out," said Stahr.

"I used to go to Malibu, but they don't like it, those moving picture people."

A wave came in and forced them back, receded swiftly, leaving the sand alive again.

"Is it worth the trip?" Stahr asked.

"I don't figure it that way. I really come out to read some Emerson. Have you ever read him?"

"I have," said Kathleen. "Some."

"I've got him inside my shirt. I got some Rosicrucian literature with me, too, but I'm fed up with them."

The wind had changed a little—the waves were stronger further down, and they walked along the foaming edge of the water.

"What's your work," the negro asked Stahr.

"I work for the pictures."

"Oh." After a moment he added, "I never go to movies."

"Why not?" asked Stahr sharply.

"There's no profit. I never let my children go."

Stahr watched him, and Kathleen watched Stahr protectively.

"Some of them are good," she said, against a wave of spray; but he did not hear her. She felt she could contradict him and said it again, and this time he looked at her indifferently.

"Are the Rosicrucian brotherhood against pictures?" asked Stahr.

"Seems as if they don't know what they *are* for. One week they for one thing and next week for another."

Only the little fish were certain. Half an hour had gone, and still they came. The negro's two pails were full, and finally he went off over the beach toward the road, unaware that he had rocked an industry.

Stahr and Kathleen walked back to the house, and she thought how to drive his momentary blues away.

"Poor old Sambo," she said.

"What?"

"Don't you call them poor old Sambo?"

"We don't call them anything especially." After a moment, he said, "They have pictures of their own."

In the house she drew on her shoes and stockings before the heater.

"I like California better," she said deliberately. "I think I was a bit sex-starved."

"That wasn't quite all, was it?"

"You know it wasn't."

"It's nice to be near you."

She gave a little sigh as she stood up, so small that he did not notice it.

"I don't want to lose you now," he said. "I don't know what you think of me or whether you think of me at all. As you've probably guessed, my heart's in the grave—" He hesitated, wondering if this was quite true. "—but you're the most attractive woman I've met since I don't know when. I can't stop looking at you. I don't know now exactly the color of your eyes, but they make me sorry for everyone in the world——"

"Stop it, stop it!" she cried laughing. "You'll have me looking in the mirror for weeks. My eyes aren't any color—they're just eyes to see with, and I'm just as ordinary as I can be. I have nice teeth for an English girl——"

"You have beautiful teeth."

"—but I couldn't hold a candle to these girls I see here——"

"*You* stop it," he said. "What I said is true, and I'm a cautious man."

She stood motionless a moment—thinking. She looked at him, then she looked back into herself, then at him again—then she gave up her thought.

"We must go," she said.

Now they were different people as they started back. Four times they had driven along the shore road today, each time a different pair. Curiosity, sadness and desire were behind them now; this was a true returning—to themselves and all their past and future and the encroaching presence of tomorrow. He asked her to sit close in the car, and she did, but they did not seem close, because for that you have to seem to be growing closer. Nothing stands still. It was on his tongue to ask her to come to the house he rented and sleep there tonight—but he felt that it would make him sound lonely. As the car climbed the hill to her house, Kathleen looked for something behind the seat cushion.

"What have you lost?"

"It might have fallen out," she said, feeling through her purse in the darkness.

"What was it?"

"An envelope."

"Was it important?"

"No."

But when they got to her house and Stahr turned on the dashboard light, she helped take the cushions out and look again.

"It doesn't matter," she said, as they walked to the door. "What's your address where you really live?"

"Just Bel-air. There's no number."

"Where is Bel-air?"

"It's a sort of development, near Santa Monica. But you'd better call me at the studio."

"All right . . . good night, Mr. Stahr."

"*Mister* Stahr," he repeated, astonished.

She corrected herself gently.

"Well, then, good night, Stahr. Is that better?"

He felt as though he had been pushed away a little.

"As you like," he said. He refused to let the aloofness communicate itself. He kept looking at her and moved his head from side to side in her own gesture, saying without words: "You know what's happened to me." She sighed. Then she came into his arms and for a moment was his again completely. Before anything could change, Stahr whispered good night and turned away and went to his car.

Winding down the hill, he listened inside himself as if something by an unknown composer, powerful and strange and strong, was about to be played for the first time. The theme would be stated presently, but because the composer was always new, he would not recognize it as the theme right away. It would come in some such guise as the auto horns from the technicolor boulevards below, or be barely audible, a tattoo on the muffled drum of the moon. He strained to hear it, knowing only that music was beginning, new music that he liked and did not understand. It was hard to react to what one could entirely compass—this was new and confusing, nothing one could shut off in the middle and supply the rest from an old score.

Also, and persistently, and bound up with the other, there was the negro on the sand. He was waiting at home for Stahr, with his pails of silver fish, and he would be waiting at the studio in the morning. He had said that he did not allow his children to listen to Stahr's story. He was prejudiced and wrong, and he must be shown somehow, some way. A picture, many pictures, a decade of pictures, must be made to show him he was wrong. Since he had spoken, Stahr had thrown four pictures out of his plans—one that was going into production this week. They were borderline pictures in point of interest, but at least he submitted the borderline pictures to the negro and found them trash. And he put back on his list a difficult picture that he had tossed to the wolves, to Brady and Marcus and the rest, to get his way on something else. He rescued it for the negro man.

When he drove up to his door, the porch lights went on, and his Philippino came down the steps to put away the car. In the library, Stahr found a list of phone calls:

"La Borwitz
Marcus
Harlow
Reinmund
Fairbanks
Brady
Colman
Skouras
Fleishacker," *etc*.

The Philippino came into the room with a letter.
"This fell out of the car," he said.
"Thanks," said Stahr. "I was looking for it."
"Will you be running a picture tonight, Mr. Stahr?"
"No, thanks—you can go to bed."
The letter, to his surprise, was addressed to Monroe Stahr, Esq.
He started to open it—then it occurred to him that she had wanted
to recapture it, and possibly to withdraw it. If she had had a phone,
he would have called her for permission before opening it. He held
it for a moment. It had been written before they met—it was odd
to think that whatever it said was now invalidated; it possessed the
interest of a souvenir by representing a mood that was gone.

Still he did not like to read it without asking her. He put it down
beside a pile of scripts and sat down with the top script in his lap.
He was proud of resisting his first impulse to open the letter. It
seemed to prove that he was not "losing his head." He had never
lost his head about Minna, even in the beginning—it had been the
most appropriate and regal match imaginable. She had loved him
always and just before she died, all unwilling and surprised, his
tenderness had burst and surged forward and he had been in love
with her. In love with Minna and death together—with the world in
which she looked so alone that he wanted to go with her there.

But "falling for dames" had never been an obsession—his brother
had gone to pieces over a dame, or rather over dame after dame after
dame. But Stahr, in his younger days, had them once and never
more than once—like one drink. He had quite another sort of adventure reserved for his mind—something better than a series of emo-

tional sprees. Like many brilliant men, he had grown up dead cold. Beginning at about twelve, probably, with the total rejection common to those of extraordinary mental powers, the "See here: this is all wrong—a mess—all a lie—and a sham—," he swept it all away, everything, as men of his type do; and then instead of being a son-of-a-bitch as most of them are, he looked around at the barrenness that was left and said to himself, "*This* will never do." And so he had learned tolerance, kindness, forbearance, and even affection like lessons.

The Philippino boy brought in a carafe of water and bowls of nuts and fruit, and said good night. Stahr opened the first script and began to read.

He read for three hours—stopping from time to time, editing without a pencil. Sometimes he looked up, warm from some vague happy thought that was not in the script, and it took him a minute each time to remember what it was. Then he knew it was Kathleen, and he looked at the letter—it was nice to have a letter.

It was three o'clock when a vein began to bump in the back of his hand, signalling that it was time to quit. Kathleen was really far away now with the waning night—the different aspects of her telescoped into the memory of a single thrilling stranger, bound to him only by a few slender hours. It seemed perfectly all right to open the letter.

"Dear Mr. Stahr.

"In half an hour I will be keeping my date with you. When we say goodbye I will hand you this letter. It is to tell you that I am to be married soon and that I won't be able to see you after today.

"I should have told you last night but it didn't seem to concern you. And it would seem silly to spend this beautiful afternoon telling you about it and watching your interest fade. Let it fade all at once —now. I will have told you enough to convince you that I am Nobody's Prize Potato. (I have just learned that expression—from my hostess of last night, who called and stayed an hour. She seems to believe that everyone is Nobody's Prize Potato—except you. I think I am supposed to tell you she thinks this, so give her a job if you can.)

"I am very flattered that anyone who sees so many lovely women—

I can't finish this sentence but you know what I mean. And I will be late if I don't go to meet you right now.

"With All Good Wishes

"KATHLEEN MOORE."

Stahr's first feeling was like fear; his first thought was that the letter was invalidated—she had even tried to retrieve it. But then he remembered "Mister Stahr" just at the end, and that she had asked him his address—she had probably already written another letter which would also say goodbye. Illogically he was shocked by the letter's indifference to what had happened later. He read it again, realizing that it foresaw nothing. Yet in front of the house she had decided to let it stand, belittling everything that had happened, curving her mind away from the fact that there had been no other man in her consciousness that afternoon. But he could not even believe this now, and the whole adventure began to peel away even as he recapitulated it searchingly to himself. The car, the hill, the hat, the music, the letter itself, blew off like the scraps of tar paper from the rubble of his house. And Kathleen departed, packing up her remembered gestures, her softly moving head, her sturdy eager body, her bare feet in the wet swirling sand. The skies paled and faded—the wind and rain turned dreary, washing the silver fish back to sea. It was only one more day, and nothing was left except the pile of scripts upon the table.

He went upstairs. Minna died again on the first landing, and he forgot her lingeringly and miserably again, step by step to the top. The empty floor stretched around him—the doors with no one sleeping behind. In his room, Stahr took off his tie, untied his shoes and sat on the side of his bed. It was all closed out, except for something that he could not remember; then he remembered: her car was still down in the parking lot of the hotel. He set his clock to give him six hours' sleep.

This is Cecilia taking up the story. I think it would be most interesting to follow my own movements at this point, as this is a time in my life that I am ashamed of. What people are ashamed of usually makes a good story.

When I sent Wylie over to Martha Dodd's table, he had no success in finding out who the girl was, but it had suddenly become my chief interest in life. Also, I guessed—correctly—that it would be Martha Dodd's. To have had at your table a girl who is admired by royalty, who may be tagged for a coronet in our little feudal system—and not even know her name!

I had only a speaking acquaintance with Martha, and it would be too obvious to approach her directly, but I went out to the studio Monday and dropped in on Jane Meloney.

Jane Meloney was quite a friend of mine. I thought of her rather as a child thinks of a family dependent. I knew she was a writer, but I grew up thinking that writer and secretary were the same, except that a writer usually smelled of cocktails and came more often to meals. They were spoken of the same way when they were not around—except for a species called playwrights, who came from the East. These were treated with respect if they did not stay long—if they did, they sank with the others into the white collar class.

Jane's office was in the "old writers' building." There was one on every lot, a row of iron maidens left over from silent days and still resounding with the dull moans of cloistered hacks and bums. There was the story of the new producer who had gone down the line one day and then reported excitedly to the head office.

"Who are those men?"

"They're supposed to be writers."

"I thought so. Well, I watched them for ten minutes and there were two of them that didn't write a line."

Jane was at her typewriter, about to break off for lunch. I told her frankly that I had a rival.

"It's a dark horse," I said. "I can't even find out her name."

"Oh," said Jane. "Well, maybe I know something about that. I heard something from somebody."

The somebody, of course, was her nephew, Ned Sollinger, Stahr's office boy. He had been her pride and hope. She had sent him through New York University, where he played on the football team. Then in his first year at medical school, after a girl turned him down, he dissected out the least publicized section of a lady corpse and sent it to the girl. Don't ask me why. In disgrace with fortune and men's eyes, he had begun life at the bottom again, and was still there.

"What do you know?" I asked.

"It was the night of the earthquake. She fell into the lake on the back lot, and he dove in and saved her life. Someone else told me it was his balcony she jumped off of and broke her arm."

"Who was she?"

"Well, that's funny, too—"

Her phone rang, and I waited restlessly during a long conversation she had with Joe Reinmund. He seemed to be trying to find out over the phone how good she was or whether she had ever written any pictures at all. And she was reputed to have been on the set the day Griffith invented the close-up! While he talked she groaned silently, writhed, made faces into the receiver, held it all in her lap so that the voice reached her faintly—and kept up a side chatter to me.

"What is *he* doing—killing time between appointments? . . . He's asked me every one of these questions ten times . . . that's all on a memorandum I sent him.". . .

And into the phone:

"If this goes up to Monroe, it won't be my doing. I want to go right through to the end."

She shut her eyes in agony again.

"Now he's casting it . . . he's casting the minor characters . . . he's going to have Buddy Ebson. . . . My God, he just hasn't anything to do . . . now he's on Walter Davenport—he means Donald Crisp . . . he's got a big casting directory open in his lap and I can hear him turn the pages . . . he's a big important man this morning, a second Stahr, and for Christ sake I've got two scenes to do before lunch."

Reinmund quit finally or was interrupted at his end. A waiter came in from the commissary with Jane's luncheon and a Coca-Cola for me—I wasn't lunching that summer. Jane wrote down one sentence on her typewriter before she ate. It interested me the way she wrote. One day I was there when she and a young man had just lifted a story out of *The Saturday Evening Post*—changing the characters and all. Then they began to write it, making each line answer the line before it, and of course it sounded just like people do in life when they're straining to be anything—funny or gentle or brave.

I always wanted to see that one on the screen, but I missed it somehow.

I found her as lovable as a cheap old toy. She made three thousand a week, and her husbands all drank and beat her nearly to death. But today I had an axe to grind.

"You don't know her name?" I persisted.

"Oh—" said Jane, "that. Well, he kept calling her up afterwards, and he told Katy Doolan it was the wrong name, after all."

"I think he found her," I said. "Do you know Martha Dodd?"

"Hasn't that little girl had a tough break, though!" she exclaimed with ready theatrical sympathy.

"Could you possibly invite her to lunch tomorrow?"

"Oh, I think she gets enough to eat all right. There's a Mexican—"

I explained that my motives were not charitable. Jane agreed to coöperate. She called Martha Dodd.

We had lunch next day at the Bev Brown Derby, a languid restaurant, patronized for its food by clients who always look as if they'd like to lie down. There is some animation at lunch, where the women put on a show for the first five minutes after they eat, but we were a tepid threesome. I should have come right out with my curiosity. Martha Dodd was an agricultural girl, who had never quite understood what had happened to her and had nothing to show for it except a washed-out look about the eyes. She still believed that the life she had tasted was reality and this was only a long waiting.

"I had a beautiful place in 1928," she told us, "—thirty acres, with a miniature golf course and a pool and a gorgeous view. All spring I was up to my ass in daisies."

I ended by asking her to come over and meet Father. This was pure penance for having had "a mixed motive" and being ashamed of it. One doesn't mix motives in Hollywood—it is confusing. Everybody understands, and the climate wears you down. A mixed motive is conspicuous waste.

Jane left us at the studio gate, disgusted by my cowardice. Martha had worked up inside to a pitch about her career—not a very high pitch, because of seven years of neglect, but a sort of nervous acquiescence, and I was going to speak strongly to Father. They never did anything for people like Martha, who had made them so much money at one time. They let them slip away into misery eked out with extra work—it would have been kinder to ship them out of town. And Father was being so proud of me this summer. I had to keep him from telling everybody just how I had been brought up so as to produce such a perfect jewel. And Bennington—oh, what an exclusive—dear God, my heart. I assured him there was the usual proportion of natural-born skivvies and biddies tastefully concealed by throw-overs from sex Fifth Avenue; but Father had worked himself up to practically an alumnus. "You've had everything," he used to say happily. Everything included roughly the two years in Florence, where I managed against heavy odds to be the only virgin in school, and the courtesy début in Boston, Massachusetts. I was a veritable flower of the fine old cost-and-gross aristocracy.

So I knew he would do something for Martha Dodd, and as we went into his office, I had great dreams of doing something for Johnny Swanson, the cowboy, too, and Evelyn Brent, and all sorts of discarded flowers. Father was a charming and sympathetic man— except for that time I had seen him unexpectedly in New York— and there was something touching about his being my father. After all, he was *my* father—he would do anything in the world for me.

Only Rosemary Schmiel was in the outer office, and she was on Birdy Peters' phone. She waved for me to sit down, but I was full of my plans and, telling Martha to take it easy, I pressed the clicker under Rosemary's desk and went toward the opened door.

"Your father's in conference," Rosemary called. "Not in conference, but I ought to——"

By this time I was through the door and a little vestibule and another door, and caught Father in his shirtsleeves, very sweaty and trying to open a window. It was a hot day, but I hadn't realized it was that hot, and thought he was ill.

"No, I'm all right," he said. "What is it?"

I told him. I told him the whole theory of people like Martha Dodd, walking up and down his office. How could he use them and guarantee them regular employment? He seemed to take me up excitedly and kept nodding and agreeing, and I felt closer to him

than I had for a long time. I came close and kissed him on his
cheek. He was trembling and his shirt was soaked through.

"You're not well," I said, "or you're in some sort of stew."

"No, I'm not at all."

"What is it?"

"Oh, it's Monroe," he said. "That goddam little Vine Street Jesus!
He's in my hair night and day!"

"What's happened?" I asked, very much cooler.

"Oh, he sits like a little goddam priest or rabbi and says what
he'll do and he won't do. I can't tell you now—I'm half crazy. Why
don't you go along?"

"I won't have you like this."

"Go along, I tell you!" I sniffed, but he never drank.

"Go and brush your hair," I said. "I want you to see Martha
Dodd."

"In here! I'd never get rid of her."

"Out there then. Go wash up first. Put on another shirt."

With an exaggerated gesture of despair, he went into the little
bathroom adjoining. It was hot in the office as if it had been closed
for hours, and maybe that was making him sick, so I opened two
more windows.

"You go along," Father called from behind the closed door of
the bathroom. "I'll be there presently."

"Be awfully nice to her," I said. "No charity."

As if it were Martha speaking for herself, a long low moan came
from somewhere in the room. I was startled—then transfixed, as it
came again, not from the bathroom where Father was, not from outside, but from a closet in the wall across from me. How I was
brave enough I don't know, but I ran across to it and opened it, and
Father's secretary, Birdy Peters, tumbled out stark naked—just like
a corpse in the movies. With her came a gust of stifling, stuffy air.
She flopped sideways on the floor, with the one hand still clutching
some clothes, and lay on the floor bathed in sweat—just as Father
came in from the bathroom. I could feel him standing behind me,
and without turning I knew exactly how he looked, for I had surprised him before.

"Cover her up," I said, covering her up myself with a rug from
the couch. "Cover her up!"

I left the office. Rosemary Schmiel saw my face as I came out and responded with a terrified expression. I never saw her again or Birdy Peters either. As Martha and I went out, Martha asked: "What's the matter, dear?"—and when I didn't say anything: "You did your best. Probably it was the wrong time. I'll tell you what I'll do. I'll take you to see a very nice English girl. Did you see the girl that Stahr danced with at our table the other night?"

So at the price of a little immersion in the family drains I had what I wanted.

I don't remember much about our call. She wasn't at home was one reason. The screen door of her house was unlocked, and Martha went in calling "Kathleen" with bright familiarity. The room we saw was bare and formal as a hotel; there were flowers about, but they did not look like sent flowers. Also, Martha found a note on the table, which said: "Leave the dress. Have gone looking for a job. Will drop by tomorrow."

Martha read it twice but it didn't seem to be for Stahr, and we waited five minutes. People's houses are very still when they are gone. Not that I expect them to be jumping around, but I leave the observation for what it's worth. Very still. Prim almost, with just a fly holding down the place and paying no attention to you, and the corner of a curtain blowing.

"I wonder what kind of a job," said Martha. "Last Sunday she went somewhere with Stahr."

But I was no longer interested. It seemed awful to be here—producer's blood, I thought in horror. And in quick panic I pulled her out into the placid sunshine. It was no use—I felt just black and awful. I had always been proud of my body—I had a way of thinking of it as geometric which made everything it did seem all right. And there was probably not any kind of place, including churches and offices and shrines where people had not embraced—but no one had ever stuffed me naked into a hole in the wall in the middle of a business day.

"If you were in a drug-store," said Stahr, "—having a prescription filled——"

"You mean a chemist's?" Boxley asked.

"If you were in a chemist's," conceded Stahr, "and you were getting a prescription for some member of your family who was very sick——"

"—Very ill?" queried Boxley.

"Very ill. *Then* whatever caught your attention through the window, whatever distracted you and held you would probably be material for pictures."

"A murder outside the window, you mean."

"There you go," said Stahr, smiling. "It might be a spider working on the pane."

"Of course—I see.'"

"I'm afraid you don't, Mr. Boxley. You see it for *your* medium, but not for ours. You keep the spiders for yourself and you try to pin the murders on us."

"I might as well leave," said Boxley. "I'm no good to you. I've been here three weeks and I've accomplished nothing. I make suggestions, but no one writes them down."

"I want you to stay. Something in you doesn't like pictures, doesn't like telling a story this way——"

"It's such a damned bother," exploded Boxley. "You can't let yourself go——"

He checked himself. He knew that Stahr, the helmsman, was finding time for him in the middle of a constant stiff blow—that they were talking in the always creaking rigging of a ship sailing in great awkward tacks along an open sea. Or else—it seemed at times—they were in a huge quarry—where even the newly-cut marble bore the tracery of old pediments, half-obliterated inscriptions of the past.

"I keep wishing you could start over," Boxley said. "It's this mass production."

"That's the condition," said Stahr. "There's always some lousy condition. We're making a life of Rubens—suppose I asked you to do portraits of rich dopes like Bill Brady and me and Gary Cooper and Marcus when you wanted to paint Jesus Christ! Wouldn't you feel you had a condition? Our condition is that we have to take people's own favorite folklore and dress it up and give it back to them. Anything beyond that is sugar. So won't you give us some sugar, Mr. Boxley?"

Boxley knew he could sit with Wylie White tonight at the Troc raging at Stahr, but he had been reading Lord Charnwood and he recognized that Stahr like Lincoln was a leader carrying on a long war on many fronts; almost single-handed he had moved pictures sharply forward through a decade, to a point where the content of the "A productions" was wider and richer than that of the stage. Stahr was an artist only, as Mr. Lincoln was a general, perforce and as a layman.

"Come down to La Borwitz' office with me," said Stahr. "They sure need some sugar there."

In La Borwitz' office, two writers, a shorthand secretary and a hushed supervisor, sat in a tense smoky stalemate, where Stahr had left them three hours before. He looked at the faces one after another and found nothing. La Borwitz spoke with awed reverence for his defeat.

"We've just got too many characters, Monroe."

Stahr snorted affably.

"That's the principal idea of the picture."

He took some change out of his pocket, looked up at the suspended light and tossed up half a dollar, which clanked into the bowl. He looked at the coins in his hands and selected a quarter.

La Borwitz watched miserably; he knew this was a favorite idea of Stahr's and he saw the sands running out. At the moment everyone's back was toward him. Suddenly he brought up his hands from their placid position under the desk and threw them high in the air, so high that they seemed to leave his wrist—and then he caught them neatly as they were descending. After that he felt better. He was in control.

One of the writers had taken out some coins, also, and presently rules were defined. "You have to toss your coin through the chains without hitting them. Whatever falls into the light is the kitty."

They played for half an hour—all except Boxley, who sat aside and dug into the script, and the secretary, who kept tally. She calculated the cost of the four men's time, arriving at a figure of sixteen hundred dollars. At the end, La Borwitz was winner by $5.50, and a janitor brought in a step-ladder to take the money out of the light.

Boxley spoke up suddenly.

"You have the stuffings of a turkey here," he said.

"What!"

"It's not pictures."

They looked at him in astonishment. Stahr concealed a smile.

"So we've got a real picture man here!" exclaimed La Borwitz.

"A lot of beautiful speeches," said Boxley boldly, "but no situations. After all, you know, it's not going to be a novel. And it's too long. I can't exactly describe how I feel, but it's not quite right. And it leaves me cold."

He was giving them back what had been handed him for three weeks. Stahr turned away, watching the others out of the corner of his eye.

"We don't need *less* characters," said Boxley. "We need *more*. As I see it, that's the idea."

"That's the idea," said the writers.

"Yes—that's the idea," said La Borwitz.

Boxley was inspired by the attention he had created.

"Let each character see himself in the other's place," he said. "The policeman is about to arrest the thief when he sees that the thief actually has *his* face. I mean, show it that way. You could almost call the thing *Put Yourself in My Place*."

Suddenly they were at work again—taking up this new theme in turn like hepcats in a swing band and going to town with it. They might throw it out again tomorrow, but life had come back for a moment. Pitching the coins had done it as much as Boxley. Stahr had recreated the proper atmosphere—never consenting to be a driver of the driven, but feeling like and acting like and even sometimes looking like a small boy getting up a show.

He left them, touching Boxley on the shoulder in passing—a deliberate accolade—he didn't want them to gang up on him and break his spirit in an hour.

Doctor Baer was waiting in his inner office. With him was a colored man with a portable cardiograph like a huge suitcase. Stahr called it the lie detector. Stahr stripped to the waist, and the weekly examination began.

"How've you been feeling?"

"Oh—the usual," said Stahr.

"Been hard at it? Getting any sleep?"

"No—about five hours. If I go to bed early, I just lie there."

"Take the sleeping pills."

"The yellow one gives me a hangover."

"Take two red ones, then."

"That's a nightmare."

"Take one of each—the yellow first."

"All right—I'll try. How've *you* been?"

"Say—I take care of myself, Monroe, I save myself."

"The hell you do—you're up all night sometimes."

"Then I sleep all next day."

After ten minutes, Baer said:

"Seems O.K. The blood pressure's up five points."

"Good," said Stahr. "That's good, isn't it?"

"That's good. I'll develop the cardiographs tonight. When are you coming away with me?"

"Oh, some time," said Stahr lightly. "In about six weeks things'll ease up."

Baer looked at him with a genuine liking that had grown over three years.

"You got better in thirty-three when you laid up," he said. "Even for three weeks."

"I will again."

No he wouldn't, Baer thought. With Minna's help he had enforced a few short rests years ago and lately he had hinted around, trying to find who Stahr considered his closest friends. Who could take him away and keep him away? It would almost surely be useless. He was due to die very soon now. Within six months one could say definitely. What was the use of developing the cardiograms? You couldn't persuade a man like Stahr to stop and lie down and look at the sky for six months. He would much rather die. He said differently, but what it added up to was the definite urge toward total exhaustion that he had run into before. Fatigue was a drug as well as a poison, and Stahr apparently derived some rare almost physical pleasure from working lightheaded with weariness. It was a perversion of the life force he had seen before, but he had almost stopped trying to interfere with it. He had cured a man or so—a hollow triumph of killing and preserving the shell.

"You hold your own," he said.

They exchanged a glance. Did Stahr know? Probably. But he did not know when—he did not know how soon now.

"If I hold my own, I can't ask more," said Stahr.

The colored man had finished packing the apparatus.

"Next week same time?"

"O.K., Bill," said Stahr. "Goodbye."

. As the door closed, Stahr switched open the dictograph. Miss Doolan's voice came through immediately.

"Do you know a Miss Kathleen Moore?"

"What do you mean?" he asked startled.

"A Miss Kathleen Moore is on the line. She said you asked her to call."

"Well, my God!" he exclaimed. He was swept with indignant rapture. It had been five days—this would never do at all.

"She's on now?"

"Yes."

"Well, all right then."

In a moment he heard the voice up close to him.

"Are you married?" he asked, low and surly.

"No, not yet."

His memory blocked out her face and form—as he sat down, she seemed to lean down to his desk, keeping level with his eyes.

"What's on your mind?" he asked in the same surly voice. It was hard to talk that way.

"You did find the letter?" she asked.

"Yes. It turned up that night."

"That's what I want to speak to you about."

He found an attitude at length—he was outraged.

"What is there to talk about?" he demanded.

"I tried to write you another letter, but it wouldn't write."

"I know that, too."

There was a pause.

"Oh, cheer up!" she said surprisingly. "This doesn't sound like you. It *is* Stahr, isn't it? That very nice Mr. Stahr?"

"I feel a little outraged," he said almost pompously. "I don't see the use of this. I had at least a pleasant memory of you."

"I don't believe it's you," she said. "Next thing you'll wish me luck." Suddenly she laughed: "Is this what you planned to say? I know how *aw*ful it gets when you plan to say anything——"

"I never expected to hear from you again," he said with dignity; but it was no use, she laughed again—a woman's laugh that is like a child's, just one syllable, a crow and a cry of delight.

"Do you know how you make me feel?" she demanded. "Like a day in London during a caterpillar plague when a hot furry thing dropped in my mouth."

"I'm sorry."

"Oh, please wake up," she begged. "I want to see you. I can't explain things on the phone. It was no fun for me either, you understand."

"I'm very busy. There's a sneak preview in Glendale tonight."

"Is that an invitation?"

"George Boxley, the English writer, is going with me." He surprised himself. "Do you want to come along?"

"How could we talk?"

She considered. "Why don't you call for me afterwards," she suggested. "We could ride around."

Miss Doolan on the huge dictograph was trying to cut in on the line with a shooting director—the only interruption ever permitted. He flipped the button and called "Wait" impatiently into the machine.

"About eleven?" Kathleen was saying confidentially.

The idea of "riding around" seemed so unwise that if he could have thought of the words to refuse her he would have spoken them, but he did not want to be the caterpillar. Suddenly he had no attitude left except the sense that the day, at least, was complete. He had an evening—a beginning, a middle and an end.

He rapped on the screen door, heard her call from inside, and stood waiting where the level fell away. From below came the whir of a lawn mower—a man was cutting his grass at midnight. The moon was so bright that Stahr could see him plainly, a hundred feet off and down, as he stopped and rested on the handle before pushing it back across his garden. There was a midsummer restlessness abroad—early August with imprudent loves and impulsive crimes.

With little more to expect from summer, one tried anxiously to live in the present—or, if there was no present, to invent one.

She came at last. She was all different and delighted. She wore a suit with a skirt that she kept hitching up as they walked down to the car with a brave, gay, stimulating, reckless air of "Tighten up your belt, baby. Let's get going." Stahr had brought his limousine with the chauffeur, and the intimacy of the four walls whisking them along a new curve in the dark took away any strangeness at once. In its way, the little trip they made was one of the best times he had ever had in his life. It was certainly one of the times when, if he knew he was going to die, it was not tonight.

She told him her story. She sat beside him cool and gleaming for a while, spinning on excitedly, carrying him to far places with her, meeting and knowing the people she had known. The story was vague at first. "This Man" was the one she had loved and lived with. "This American" was the one who had rescued her when she was sinking into a quicksand.

"Who is he—the American?"

Oh, names—what did they matter? No one important like Stahr, not rich. He had lived in London and now they would live out here. She was going to be a good wife, a real person. He was getting a divorce—not just on account of her—but that was the delay.

"But the first man?" asked Stahr. "How did you get into that?"

Oh, that was a blessing at first. From sixteen to twenty-one the thing was to eat. The day her stepmother presented her at Court they had one shilling to eat with so as not to feel faint. Sixpence apiece, but the stepmother watched while she ate. After a few months the stepmother died, and she would have sold out for that shilling but she was too weak to go into the streets. London can be harsh—oh, quite.

Was there nobody?

There were friends in Ireland who sent butter. There was a soup kitchen. There was a visit to an uncle, who made advances to her when she had a full stomach, and she held out and got fifty pounds out of him for not telling his wife.

"Couldn't you work?" Stahr asked.

"I worked. I sold cars. Once I sold a car."

"But couldn't you get a regular job?"

"It's hard—it's different. There was a feeling that people like me forced other people out of jobs. A woman struck me when I tried to get a job as chambermaid in a hotel."

"But you were presented at Court?"

"That was my stepmother who did that—on an off chance. I was nobody. My father was shot by the Black-and-Tans in twenty-two when I was a child. He wrote a book called *Last Blessing*. Did you ever read it?"

"I don't read."

"I wish you'd buy it for the movies. It's a good little book. I still get a royalty from it—ten shillings a year."

Then she met "The Man" and they travelled the world around. She had been to all the places that Stahr made movies of, and lived in cities whose name he had never heard. Then The Man went to seed, drinking and sleeping with the housemaids and trying to force her off on his friends. They all tried to make her stick with him. They said she had saved him and should cleave to him longer now, indefinitely, to the end. It was her duty. They brought enormous pressure to bear. But she had met The American, and so finally she ran away.

"You should have run away before."

"Well, you see, it was difficult." She hesitated, and plunged. "You see, I ran away from a king."

His moralities somehow collapsed—she had managed to top him. A confusion of thoughts raced through his head—one of them a faint old credo that all royalty was diseased.

"It wasn't the King of England," she said. "My king was out of a job as he used to say. There are lots of kings in London." She laughed —then added almost defiantly, "He was very attractive until he began drinking and raising hell."

"What was he king of?"

She told him—and Stahr visualized the face out of old newsreels.

"He was a very learned man," she said. "He could have taught all sorts of subjects. But he wasn't much like a king. Not nearly as much as you. None of them were."

This time Stahr laughed.

"You know what I mean. They all felt old-fashioned. Most of them tried so hard to keep up with things. They were always advised to keep up with things. One was a syndicalist, for instance. And one used to carry around a couple of clippings about a tennis tournament when he was in the semi-finals. I saw those clippings a dozen times."

They rode through Griffith Park and out past the dark studios of Burbank, past the airports, and along the way to Pasadena past the neon signs of roadside cabarets. Up in his head he wanted her, but it was late and just the ride was an overwhelming joy. They held hands and once she came close into his arms saying, "Oh, you're *so* nice. I *do* like to be with you." But her mind was divided—this was not his night as the Sunday afternoon had been his. She was absorbed in herself, stung into excitement by telling of her own adventures; he could not help wondering if he was getting the story she had saved up for The American.

"How long have you known The American?" he asked.

"Oh, I knew him for several months. We used to meet. We understand each other. He used to say, 'It looks like a cinch from now on.'"

"Then why did you call me up?"

She hesitated.

"I wanted to see you once more. Then, *too*—he was supposed to arrive today, but last night he wired that he'd be another week. I wanted to talk to a friend—after all, you *are* my friend."

He wanted her very much now, but one part of his mind was cold and kept saying: She wants to see if I'm in love with her, if I want to marry her. Then she'd consider whether or not to throw this man over. She won't consider it till I've committed myself.

"Are you in love with The American?" he asked.

"Oh, yes. It's absolutely arranged. He saved my life and my reason. He's moving half-way around the world for me. I insisted on that."

"But are you in love with him?"

"Oh, yes. I'm in love with him."

The "Oh, yes" told him she was not—told him to speak for himself—that she would see. He took her in his arms and kissed her deliberately on the mouth and held her for a long time. It was so warm.

"Not tonight," she whispered.

"All right."

They passed over suicide bridge with the high new wire.

"I know what it is," she said, "but how stupid. English people don't kill themselves when they don't get what they want."

They turned around in the driveway of a hotel and started back. It was a dark night with no moon. The wave of desire had passed and neither spoke for awhile. Her talk of kings had carried him oddly back in flashes to the pearly White Way of Main Street in Erie, Pennsylvania, when he was fifteen. There was a restaurant with lobsters in the window and green weeds and bright lights on a shell cavern, and beyond behind a red curtain the terribly strange brooding mystery of people and violin music. That was just before he left for New York. This girl reminded him of the fresh iced fish and lobsters in the window. She was Beautiful Doll. Minna had never been Beautiful Doll.

They looked at each other and her eyes asked, "Shall I marry The American?" He did not answer. After awhile he said:

"Let's go somewhere for the week-end."

She considered.

"Are you talking about tomorrow?"

"I'm afraid I am."

"Well, I'll tell you tomorrow," she said.

"Tell me tonight. I'd be afraid——"

"—find a note in the car?" she laughed. "No there's no note in the car. You know almost everything now."

"Almost everything."

"Yes—almost. A few little things."

He would have to know what they were. She would tell him tomorrow. He doubted—he wanted to doubt—if there had been a maze of philandering: a fixation had held her to The Man, the king, firmly and long. Three years of a highly anomalous position—one foot in the palace and one in the background. "You had to laugh a lot," she said. "I learned to laugh a lot."

"He could have married you—like Mrs. Simpson," Stahr said in protest.

"Oh, he was married. And he wasn't a romantic." She stopped herself.

"Am I?"

"Yes," she said unwillingly, as if she were laying down a trump. "Part of you is. You're three or four different men but each of them out in the open. Like all Americans."

"Don't start trusting Americans too implicitly," he said smiling. "They may be out in the open, but they change very fast."

She looked concerned.

"Do they?"

"Very fast and all at once," he said, "and nothing ever changes them back."

"You frighten me. I always had a great sense of security with Americans."

She seemed suddenly so alone that he took her hand.

"Where will we go tomorrow?" he said. "Maybe up in the mountains. I've got everything to do tomorrow, but I won't do any of it. We can start at four and get there by afternoon."

"I'm not sure. I seem to be a little mixed up. This doesn't seem to be quite the girl who came out to California for a new life."

He could have said it then, said, "It *is* a new life," for he knew it was, he knew he could not let her go now; but something else said to sleep on it as an adult, no romantic. And not to tell her till tomorrow. Still she was looking at him, her eyes wandering from his forehead to his chin and back again, and then up and down once more, with that odd slowly-waving motion of her head.

. . . It is your chance, Stahr. Better take it now. This is your girl. She can save you, she can worry you back to life. She will take looking after and you will grow strong to do it. But take her now—tell her and take her away. Neither of you knows it, but far away over the night The American has changed his plans. At this moment his train is speeding through Albuquerque; the schedule is accurate. The engineer is on time. In the morning he will be here.

. . . The chauffeur turned up the hill to Kathleen's house. It seemed warm even in darkness—wherever he had been near here was by way of being an enchanted place for Stahr: this limousine, the rising house at the beach, the very distances they had already covered together over the sprawled city. The hill they climbed now gave forth a sort of glow, a sustained sound that struck his soul alert with delight.

As he said goodbye he felt again that it was impossible to leave her, even for a few hours. There were only ten years between them, but he felt that madness about it akin to the love of an aging man for a young girl. It was a deep and desperate time-need, a clock ticking with his heart, and it urged him, against the whole logic of his life, to walk past her into the house now and say, "This is forever."

Kathleen waited, irresolute herself—pink and silver frost waiting to melt with spring. She was a European, humble in the face of power, but there was a fierce self-respect that would only let her go so far. She had no illusions about the considerations that swayed princes.

"We'll go to the mountains tomorrow," said Stahr. Many thousands of people depended on his balanced judgment—you can suddenly blunt a quality you have lived by for twenty years.

He was very busy the next morning, Saturday. At two o'clock, when he came from luncheon, there was a stack of telegrams—a company ship was lost in the Arctic; a star was in disgrace; a writer was suing for one million dollars. Jews were dead miserably beyond the sea. The last telegram stared up at him:

I was married at noon today. Goodbye; and on a sticker attached, *Send your answer by Western Union Telegram.*

CHAPTER VI

I KNEW NOTHING about any of this. I went up to Lake Louise, and when I came back didn't go near the studio. I think I would have started East in mid-August—if Stahr hadn't called me up one day at home.

"I want you to arrange something, Cecilia—I want to meet a Communist Party member."

"Which one?" I asked, somewhat startled.

"Any one."

"Haven't you got plenty out there?"

"I mean one of their organizers—from New York."

The summer before I had been all politics—I could probably have arranged a meeting with Harry Bridges. But my boy had been killed in an auto accident after I went back to college, and I was out of touch with such things. I had heard there was a man from *The New Masses* around somewhere.

"Will you promise him immunity?" I asked, joking.

"Oh, yes," Stahr answered seriously. "I won't hurt him. Get one that can talk—tell him to bring one of his books along."

He spoke as if he wanted to meet a member of the "I am" cult.

"Do you want a blonde or a brunette?"

"Oh, get a man," he said hastily.

Hearing Stahr's voice cheered me up—since I had barged in on Father it had all seemed a paddling about in thin spittle. Stahr changed everything about it—changed the angle from which I saw it, changed the very air.

"I don't think your father ought to know," he said. "Can we pretend the man is a Bulgarian musician or something?"

"Oh, they don't dress up any more," I said.

It was harder to arrange than I thought—Stahr's negotiations with the Writers' Guild, which had continued over a year, were approaching a dead end. Perhaps they were afraid of being corrupted, and I was asked what Stahr's "proposition" was. Afterwards Stahr told me that he prepared for the meeting by running off the Russian Revolutionary films that he had in his film library at home. He also ran off *Doctor Caligari* and Salvator Dali's *Le Chien Andalou,* possibly suspecting that they had a bearing on the matter. He had been startled by the Russian films back in the twenties, and on Wylie White's suggestion he had had the script department get him up a two-page "treatment" of the *Communist Manifesto.*

But his mind was closed on the subject. He was a rationalist who did his own reasoning without benefit of books—and he had just managed to climb out of a thousand years of Jewry into the late eighteenth century. He could not bear to see it melt away—he cherished the parvenu's passionate loyalty to an imaginary past.

The meeting took place in what I called the "processed leather room"—it was one of six done for us by a decorator from Sloane's years ago, and the term stuck in my head. It was *the* most decorator's room: an angora wool carpet the color of dawn, the most delicate grey imaginable—you hardly dared walk on it; and the silver panelling and leather tables and creamy pictures and slim fragilities looked so easy to stain that we could not breathe hard in there, though it was wonderful to look into from the door when the windows were open and the curtains whimpered querulously against the breeze. It was a lineal descendant of the old American parlor that used to be closed except on Sunday. But it was exactly the room for the occasion, and I hoped that whatever happened would give it character and make it henceforth part of our house.

Stahr arrived first. He was white and nervous and troubled—except for his voice, which was always quiet and full of consideration. There was a brave personal quality in the way he would meet you—he would walk right up to you and put aside something that was in the way, and grow to know you all over as if he couldn't help himself. I kissed him for some reason, and took him into the processed leather room.

"When do you go back to college?" he asked.

We had been over this fascinating ground before.

"Would you like me if I were a little shorter?" I asked, "I could wear low heels and plaster down my hair."

"Let's have dinner tonight," he suggested. "People will think I'm your father but I don't mind."

"I *love* old men," I assured him. "Unless the man has a crutch, I feel it's just a boy and girl affair."

"Have you had many of those?"

"Enough."

"People fall in and out of love all the time, don't they?"

"Every three years or so, Fanny Brice says. I just read it in the paper."

"I wonder how they manage it," he said. "I know it's true because I see them. But they look so con*vinced* every time. And then suddenly they don't look convinced. But they get convinced all over."

"You've been making too many movies."

"I wonder if they're as convinced the second time or the third time or the fourth time," he persisted.

"More each time," I said. "Most of all the last time."

He thought this over and seemed to agree.

"I suppose so. Most of all the last time."

I didn't like the way he said this, and I suddenly saw that under the surface he was miserable.

"It's a great nuisance," he said. "It'll be better when it's over."

"Wait a *min*ute! Perhaps pictures are in the wrong hands."

Brimmer, the Party Member, was announced, and going to meet him I slid over to the door on one of those gossamer throw-rugs and practically into his arms.

He was a nice-looking man, this Brimmer—a little on the order of Spencer Tracy, but with a stronger face and a wider range of reactions written up in it. I couldn't help thinking as he and Stahr smiled and shook hands and squared off, that they were two of the most alert men I had ever seen. They were very conscious of each other immediately—both as polite to me as you please, but with a softening of the ends of their sentences when they turned in my direction.

"What are you people trying to do?" demanded Stahr. "You've got my young men all upset."

"That keeps them awake, doesn't it?" said Brimmer.

"First we let half a dozen Russians study the plant," said Stahr. "As a model plant, you understand. And then you try to break up the unity that makes it a model plant."

"The unity?" Brimmer repeated. "Do you mean what's known as The Company Spirit?"

"Oh, not that," said Stahr, impatiently. "It seems to be *me* you're after. Last week a writer came into my office—a drunk—a man who's been floating around for years just two steps out of the bughouse—and began telling me my business."

Brimmer smiled.

"You don't look to me like a man who could be told his business, Mr. Stahr."

They would both have tea. When I came back, Stahr was telling a story about the Warner Brothers and Brimmer was laughing with him.

"I'll tell you another one," Stahr said. "Balanchine the Russian Dancer had them mixed up with the Ritz Brothers. He didn't know which ones he was training and which ones he was working for. He used to go around saying, 'I cannot train these Warner Brothers to dance.'"

It looked like a quiet afternoon. Brimmer asked him why the producers didn't back the anti-Nazi League.

"Because of you people," said Stahr. "It's your way of getting at the writers. In the long view you're wasting your time. Writers are children—even in normal times they can't keep their minds on their work."

"They're the farmers in this business," said Brimmer pleasantly. "They grow the grain but they're not in at the feast. Their feeling toward the producer is like the farmers' resentment of the city fellow."

I was wondering about Stahr's girl—whether it was all over between them. Later, when I heard the whole thing from Kathleen, standing in the rain in a wretched road called Goldwyn Avenue, I figured out that this must have been a week after she sent him the telegram. She couldn't help the telegram. The man got off the train unexpectedly and walked her to the registry office without a flicker of doubt that this was what she wanted. It was eight in the morning, and Kathleen was in such a daze that she was chiefly concerned about how to get the telegram to Stahr. In theory you could stop and say, "Listen, I forgot to tell you but I met a man." But this track had been laid down so thoroughly, with such confidence, such struggle, such relief, that when it came along, suddenly cutting across the other, she found herself on it like a car on a closed switch. He watched her write the telegram, looking directly at it across the table, and she hoped he couldn't read upside down. . . .

When my mind came back into the room, they had destroyed the poor writers—Brimmer had gone so far as to admit they were "unstable."

"They are not equipped for authority," said Stahr. "There is no substitute for will. Sometimes you have to fake will when you don't feel it at all."

"I've had that experience."

"You have to say, 'It's got to be like this—no other way'—even if you're not sure. A dozen times a week that happens to me. Situations where there is no real reason for anything. You pretend there is."

"All leaders have felt that," said Brimmer. "Labor leaders, and certainly military leaders."

"So I've had to take an attitude in this Guild matter. It looks to me like a try for power, and all I am going to give the writers is money."

"You give some of them very little money. Thirty dollars a week."

"Who gets that?" asked Stahr, surprised.

"The ones that are commodities and easy to replace."

"Not on my lot," said Stahr.

"Oh, yes," said Brimmer. "Two men in your shorts department get thirty dollars a week."

"Who?"

"Man named Ransome—man named O'Brien."

Stahr and I smiled together.

"Those are not writers," said Stahr. "Those are cousins of Cecilia's father."

"There are some in other studios," said Brimmer.

Stahr took his teaspoon and poured himself some medicine from a little bottle.

"What's a fink?" he asked suddenly.

"A fink? That's a strikebreaker or a company tec."

"I thought so," said Stahr. "I've got a fifteen hundred dollar writer that every time he walks through the commissary keeps saying 'Fink!' behind other writers' chairs. If he didn't scare hell out of them, it'd be funny."

Brimmer laughed.

"I'd like to see that," he said.

"You wouldn't like to spend a day with me over there?" suggested Stahr.

Brimmer laughed with genuine amusement.

"No, Mr. Stahr. But I don't doubt but that I'd be impressed. I've heard you're one of the hardest working and most efficient men in the entire West. It'd be a privilege to watch you, but I'm afraid I'll have to deny myself."

Stahr looked at me.

"I like your friend," he said. "He's crazy, but I like him." He looked closely at Brimmer: "Born on this side?"

"Oh, yes. Several generations."

"Many of them like you?"

"My father was a Baptist minister."

"I mean are many of them Reds. I'd like to meet this big Jew that tried to blow over the Ford factory. What's his name—"

"Frankensteen?"

"That's the man. I guess some of you believe in it."

"Quite a few," said Brimmer dryly.

"Not you," said Stahr.

A shade of annoyance floated across Brimmer's face.

"Oh, yes," he said.

"Oh, no," said Stahr. "Maybe you did once."

Brimmer shrugged his shoulders.

"Perhaps the boot's on the other foot," he said. "At the bottom of your heart, Mr. Stahr, you know I'm right."

"No," said Stahr, "I think it's a bunch of tripe."

"—you think to yourself, 'He's right,' but you think the system will last out your time."

"You don't really think you're going to overthrow the government."

"No, Mr. Stahr. But we think perhaps you are."

They were nicking at each other—little pricking strokes like men

do sometimes. Women do it, too; but it is a joined battle then with
no quarter. But it is not pleasant to watch men do it, because you
never know what's next. Certainly it wasn't improving the tonal
associations of the room for me, and I moved them out the French
window into our golden-yellow California garden.

It was midsummer, but fresh water from the gasping sprinklers
made the lawn glitter like spring. I could see Brimmer look at it
with a sigh in his glance—a way they have. He opened up big
outside—inches taller than I thought and broad-shouldered. He
reminded me a little of Superman when he takes off his spectacles.
I thought he was as attractive as men can be who don't really care
about women as such. We played a round robin game of ping-pong,
and he handled his bat well. I heard Father come into the house
singing that damn *Little Girl, You've Had a Busy Day,* and then
breaking off, as if he remembered we weren't speaking any more.
It was half past six—my car was standing in the drive, and I suggested we go down to the Trocadero for dinner.

Brimmer had that look that Father O'Ney had that time in New
York when he turned his collar around and went with father and
me to the Russian Ballet. He hadn't quite ought to be here. When
Bernie, the photographer, who was waiting there for some big game
or other, came up to our table, he looked trapped—Stahr made
Bernie go away, and I would like to have had the picture.

Then, to my astonishment, Stahr had three cocktails, one after
the other.

"Now I know you've been disappointed in love," I said.

"What makes you think that, Cecilia?"

"Cocktails."

"Oh, I never drink, Cecilia. I get dyspepsia—I've never been
tight."

I counted them: "—two—*three.*"

"I didn't realize. I couldn't taste them. I thought there was something the matter."

A silly glassy look darted into his eye—then passed away.

"This is my first drink in a week," said Brimmer. "I did my drinking in the Navy."

The look was back in Stahr's eye—he winked fatuously at me
and said:

"This soap-box son-of-a-bitch has been working on the Navy."

Brimmer didn't know quite how to take this. Evidently he decided to include it with the evening, for he smiled faintly, and I saw Stahr was smiling, too. I was relieved when I saw it was safely in the great American tradition, and I tried to take hold of the conversation, but Stahr seemed suddenly all right.

"Here's my typical experience," he said very succinctly and clearly to Brimmer. "The best director in Hollywood—a man I never interfere with—has some streak in him that wants to slip a pansy into every picture, or something on that order. Something offensive. He stamps it in deep like a watermark so I can't get it out. Every time he does it the Legion of Decency moves a step forward, and something has to be sacrificed out of some honest film."

"Typical organization trouble," agreed Brimmer.

"Typical," said Stahr. "It's an endless battle. So now this director tells me it's all right because he's got a Director's Guild and I can't oppress the poor. That's how you add to my troubles."

"It's a little remote from us," said Brimmer smiling. "I don't think we'd make much headway with the directors."

"The directors used to be my pals," said Stahr proudly.

It was like Edward the Seventh's boast that he had moved in the best society in Europe.

"But some of them have never forgiven me," he continued, "for bringing out stage directors when sound came in. It put them on their toes and made them learn their jobs all over, but they never did really forgive me. That time we imported a whole new hogshead full of writers, and I thought they were great fellows till they all went red."

Gary Cooper came in and sat down in a corner with a bunch of men who breathed whenever he did and looked as if they lived off him and weren't budging. A woman across the room looked around and turned out to be Carole Lombard—I was glad that Brimmer was at least getting an eyeful.

Stahr ordered a whiskey and soda and, almost immediately, another. He ate nothing but a few spoonfuls of soup and he said all the awful things about everybody being lazy so-and-so's and none of it mattered to *him* because he had lots of money—it was the kind of talk you heard whenever Father and his friends were together.

I think Stahr realized that it sounded pretty ugly outside of the proper company—maybe he had never heard how it sounded before. Anyhow he shut up and drank off a cup of black coffee. I loved him, and what he said didn't change that, but I hated Brimmer to carry off this impression. I wanted him to see Stahr as a sort of technological virtuoso, and here Stahr had been playing the wicked overseer to a point he would have called trash if he had watched it on the screen.

"I'm a production man," he said, as if to modify his previous attitude. "I like writers—I think I understand them. I don't want to kick anybody out if they do their work."

"We don't want you to," said Brimmer pleasantly. "We'd like to take you over as a going concern."

Stahr nodded grimly.

"I'd like to put you in a roomful of my partners. They've all got a dozen reasons for having Fitts run you fellows out of town."

"We appreciate your protection," said Brimmer with a certain irony. "Frankly we *do* find you difficult, Mr. Stahr—precisely because you are a paternalistic employer and your influence is very great."

Stahr was only half listening.

"I never thought," he said, "that I had more brains than a writer has. But I always thought that his brains be*longed* to me—because I knew how to use them. Like the Romans—I've heard that they never invented things but they knew what to do with them. Do you see? I don't say it's right. But it's the way I've always felt—since I was a boy."

This interested Brimmer—the first thing that had interested him for an hour.

"You know yourself very well, Mr. Stahr," he said.

I think he wanted to get away. He had been curious to see what kind of man Stahr was, and now he thought he knew. Still hoping things would be different, I rashly urged him to ride home with us, but when Stahr stopped by the bar for another drink I knew I'd made a mistake.

It was a gentle, harmless, motionless evening with a lot of Saturday cars. Stahr's hand lay along the back of the seat touching my hair. Suddenly I wished it had been about ten years ago—I would have been nine, Brimmer about eighteen and working his

way through some mid-western college, and Stahr twenty-five, just
having inherited the world and full of confidence and joy. We would
both have looked up to Stahr so, without question. And here we were
in an adult conflict, to which there was no peaceable solution, complicated now with exhaustion and drink.

We turned in at our drive, and I drove around to the garden
again.

"I must go along now," said Brimmer. "I've got to meet some
people."

"No, stay," said Stahr. "I never have said what I wanted. We'll
play ping-pong and have another drink, and then we'll tear into
each other."

Brimmer hesitated. Stahr turned on the floodlight and picked up
his ping-pong bat, and I went into the house for some whiskey—
I wouldn't have dared disobey him.

When I came back, they were not playing, but Stahr was batting
a whole box of new balls across to Brimmer, who turned them aside.
When I arrived, he quit and took the bottle and retired to a chair
just out of the floodlight, watching in dark dangerous majesty. He
was pale—he was so transparent that you could almost watch the
alcohol mingle with the poison of his exhaustion.

"Time to relax on Saturday night," he said.

"You're not relaxing," I said.

He was carrying on a losing battle with his instinct toward
schizophrenia.

"I'm going to beat up Brimmer," he announced after a moment.
"I'm going to handle this thing personally."

"Can't you pay somebody to do it?" asked Brimmer.

I signalled him to keep quiet.

"I do my own dirty work," said Stahr. "I'm going to beat hell
out of you and put you on a train."

He got up and came forward, and I put my arms around him,
gripping him.

"Please *stop* this!" I said. "Oh, you're being so bad."

"This fellow has an influence over you," he said darkly. "Over all
you young people. You don't know what you're doing."

"Please go home," I said to Brimmer.

Stahr's suit was made of slippery cloth and suddenly he slipped away from me and went for Brimmer. Brimmer retreated backward around the table. There was an odd expression in his face, and afterwards I thought it looked as if he were saying, "Is *this* all? This frail half-sick person holding up the whole thing."

Then Stahr came close, his hands going up. It seemed to me that Brimmer held him off with his left arm a minute, and then I looked away—I couldn't bear to watch.

When I looked back, Stahr was out of sight below the level of the table, and Brimmer was looking down at him.

"Please go home," I said to Brimmer.

"All right." He stood looking down at Stahr as I came around the table. "I always wanted to hit ten million dollars, but I didn't know it would be like this."

Stahr lay motionless.

"Please go," I said.

"I'm sorry. Can I help——"

"No. Please go. I understand."

He looked again, a little awed at the depths of Stahr's repose, which he had created in a split second. Then he went quickly away over the grass, and I knelt down and shook Stahr. After a moment he came awake with a terrific convulsion and bounced up on his feet.

"Where is he?" he shouted.

"Who?" I asked innocently.

"That American. Why in hell did you have to marry him, you damn fool?"

"Monroe—he's gone. I didn't marry anybody."

I pushed him down in a chair.

"He's been gone half an hour," I lied.

The ping-pong balls lay around in the grass like a constellation of stars. I turned on a sprinkler and came back with a wet handkerchief, but there was no mark on Stahr—he must have been hit in the side of the head. He went off behind some trees and was sick, and I heard him kicking up some earth over it. After that he seemed all right, but he wouldn't go into the house till I got him some mouthwash, so I took back the whiskey bottle and got a mouthwash bottle. His wretched essay at getting drunk was over. I've been out with college freshmen, but for sheer ineptitude and absence of the

Bacchic spirit it unquestionably took the cake. Every bad thing happened to him, but that was all.

We went in the house; the cook said Father and Mr. Marcus and Fleishacker were on the veranda, so we stayed in the "processed leather room." We both sat down in a couple of places and seemed to slide off, and finally I sat on a fur rug and Stahr on a footstool beside me.

"Did I hit him?" he asked.

"Oh, yes," I said. "Quite badly."

"I don't believe it." After a minute he added: "I didn't want to hurt him. I just wanted to chase him out. I guess he got scared and hit me."

If this was his interpretation of what had happened, it was all right with me.

"Do you hold it against him?"

"Oh, no," he said. "I was drunk." He looked around. "I've never been in here before—who did this room?—somebody from the studio?"

"Somebody from New York."

"Well, I'll have to get you out of here," he said in his old pleasant way. "How would you like to go out to Doug Fairbanks' ranch and spend the night?" he asked me. "I know he'd love to have you."

That's how the two weeks started that he and I went around together. It only took one of them for Louella to have us married.

The manuscript stops at this point. The following synopsis of the rest of the story has been put together from Fitzgerald's notes and outlines and from the reports of persons with whom he discussed his work:

Soon after his interview with Brimmer, Stahr makes a trip East. A wage-cut has been threatened in the studio, and Stahr has gone to talk to the stockholders—presumably with the idea of inducing them to retrench in some other way. He and Brady have long been working at cross-purposes, and the struggle between them for the control of the company is rapidly coming to a climax. We do not know about the results of this trip from the business point of view, but, whether or not on a business errand, Stahr for the first time visits Washington with the intention of seeing the city; and it is to be presumed that the author had meant to return here to the motif introduced in the first chapter with the visit of the Hollywood people to the home of Andrew Jackson and their failure to gain admittance or even to see the place clearly: the relation of the moving-picture industry to the American ideals and tradition. It is mid-summer; Washington is stifling; Stahr comes down with summer grippe and goes around the city in a daze of fever and heat. He never succeeds in becoming acquainted with it as he had hoped to.

When he recovers and gets back to Hollywood, he finds that Brady has taken advantage of his absence to put through a fifty percent pay-cut. Brady had called a meeting of writers and told them in a tearful speech that he and the other executives would take a cut themselves if the writers would consent to take one. If they would agree, it would not be necessary to reduce the salaries of the stenographers and the other low-paid employees. The writers had accepted this arrangement, but had then been double-crossed by Brady, who had proceeded to slash the stenographers just the same. Stahr is revolted by this; and he and Brady have a violent falling-out. Stahr, though opposed to the unions, believing that any enterprising office-boy can make his way to the top as he has done, is an old-fashioned paternalistic employer, who likes to feel that the people who work for him are contented, and that he and they are on friendly terms. On the other hand, he quarrels also with Wylie White, who he finds has become truculently hostile to him, in spite of the fact that Stahr was not personally responsible for the pay-cut. Stahr has been patient in the past with White's drinking and his practical jokes, and he is hurt that the writer should not feel toward him the same kind of personal loyalty—which is the only solidarity that Stahr understands in the field of business relations.

"The Reds see him now as a conservative—Wall Street as a Red." But he finds himself driven by the logic of the situation to fall in with the idea which has been proposed and is heartily approved by Brady, of setting up a company union.

As for his own position in the studio, he had in Washington already thought of quitting; but, intimately involved in the struggle, ill, unhappy and embittered though he is, it is difficult for him to surrender to Brady. In the meantime, he has been going around with Cecilia. The girl in a conversation with her father about the attentions Stahr has apparently been paying her, has carelessly let Brady know that Stahr is in love with someone else. Brady finds out about Kathleen, whom Stahr has been seeing again, and attempts to blackmail Stahr. Stahr in disgust with the Bradys abruptly drops Cecilia. He on his side has known for years—having learned it by way of his wife's trained nurse—that Brady had had a hand in the death of the husband of a woman with whom he (Brady) had been in love. The two men threaten one another with no really conclusive evidence on either side.

But Brady has an instrument ready to his hand. The man whom Kathleen has married—whose name is W. Bronson Smith—is a technician working in the studios, who has been taking an active part in his union. It is impossible to tell precisely how Scott Fitzgerald imagined the labor situation in Hollywood for the purposes of his story. At the time of which he is writing, the various kinds of technicians had already been organized in the International Alliance of Theatrical Stage Employees; and it is obvious that he intended to exploit the element of racketeering and gangsterism revealed in this organization by the case of William Bioff. Brady was to go to Kathleen's husband and play upon his jealousy of his wife. We do not know what Fitzgerald intended that these two should try to do to Stahr. Robinson, the cutter (see the notes on this character), was originally to have undertaken to murder him; but it seems more probable from the author's outline that Stahr was to be caught in some trap which would supply Kathleen's husband with grounds for bringing a suit against Stahr for alienation of his wife's affection. In Fitzgerald's outline below, the theme of Chapter VIII is indicated by the words, "The suit and the price." This is evidently partly explained by the following note of material which Fitzgerald intended to make use of, though it is impossible to tell how it was to be modified to meet the demands of the story: "One of the ——— brothers is accused by an employee of seducing his wife. Sued for alienation. They try to settle it out of court, but the man bringing suit is a labor leader and won't be bought. Neither will he divorce his wife. He considers rougher measures. His price is that ——— shall go away for a year. ———'s instinct is to stay and fight it, but the other brothers get to a doctor and pronounce death sentence on him and retire him. He tries to get the girl to go with him, but is afraid of the Mann Act. She is to follow him and they'll go abroad."

In any case, Stahr is to be saved by the intervention of the camera man, Pete Zavras, whom he has befriended at the beginning of the story, when Zavras had lost his standing with the studios.

In the meantime, Stahr is now seriously ill. He and Kathleen have been "taking breathless chances." They have succeeded in having "one last fling," which has taken place during an overpowering heat wave in the early part of September. But their meetings have proved unsatisfactory. The author has indicated in an early sketch that Kathleen was to "come of very humble parents"—her father was to have been the captain of a Newfoundland fishing smack; and in another place he says that Stahr has found it difficult to accept her as a permanent part of his life because she is "poor, unfortunate, and tagged with a middle-class exterior which doesn't fit in with the grandeur Stahr demands of life." It is possible that the labor conflict in which her husband has become involved was intended to alienate her and Stahr. Stahr is now being pushed into the past by Brady and by the unions alike. The split between the controllers of the movie industry, on the one hand, and the various groups of employees, on the other, is widening and leaving no place for real individualists of business like Stahr, whose successes are personal achievements and whose career has always been invested with a certain personal glamor. He has held himself directly responsible to everyone with whom he has worked; he has even wanted to beat up his enemies himself. In Hollywood he is "the last tycoon."

Stahr has not been afraid, as we have seen in the conference in Chapter III, to risk money on unpopular films which would afford him some artistic satisfaction. He has had a craftsman's interest in the pictures, and it has been natural for him to want to make them better. But he has been "lying low" since the wage-cut and has ceased to make pictures altogether. There was to have been a second series of scenes showing him at a story conference, at the rushes and on the sets, which was to have contrasted with the similar series in Chapters III and IV, and to have shown the change that has taken place in his attitude and status.

He must, however, stand up to Brady, who he knows will stop at nothing. He evidently fears Brady will murder him, for he now decides to resort to Brady's own methods and get his partner murdered. For this he apparently goes straight to the gangsters. It is not clear how the murder is to be accomplished; but in order to be away at the time, Stahr arranges a trip to New York. He sees Kathleen for the last time at the airport, and also meets Cecilia, who is going back to college on a different plane. On the plane he has a reaction of disgust against the course he has taken; he realizes that he has let himself be degraded to the same plane of brutality as Brady. He decides to call off the murder and intends to wire orders as soon as the plane descends at the next airport. But the plane has an accident and crashes before they reach the next stop. Stahr is killed, and the murder goes through. The ominous suicide of Schwartz in the opening chapter of the story is thus balanced by the death of Stahr. In the note that Schwartz had sent him, he had been trying to warn him against Brady, who had long wanted to get Stahr out of the company.

Stahr's funeral, which was to have been described in detail, is an orgy of Hollywood servility and hypocrisy. Everybody is weeping copiously or conspicuously stifling emotion with an eye on the right people. Cecilia imagines Stahr present and can hear him saying "Trash!" The old cowboy actor, Johnny Swanson, who has been mentioned at the beginning of Chapter II and for whom in his forlorn situation Cecilia has later had the idea of trying to do something at the time of her visit to her father's office, has been invited to the funeral by mistake—through the confusion of his name with someone else's,—and asked to officiate as pall-bearer along with the most intimate and important of the dead producer's friends. Johnny goes through with the ceremony, rather dazed; and then finds out, to his astonishment, that his fortunes have been gloriously restored. From this time on, he is deluged with offers of jobs.

In the meantime, a final glimpse of Fleishacker, the ambitious company lawyer, a man totally without conscience or creative brains, was to have shown him as prefiguring the immediate future of the moving-picture business. There was also to have been a passage toward the end between Fleishacker and Cecilia, in which the former, who has been to New York University and who was perhaps to have tried to marry Cecilia, was to have attempted a conversation with her on an "intellectual" plane.

Cecilia, on the rebound from Stahr, has had an affair with a man she does not love—probably Wylie White, who has been after her from the first and who represents the opposition to Stahr. As a result of the death of Stahr and the murder of her father, she now breaks down completely. She develops tuberculosis, and we were to learn for the first time at the end that she has been putting together her story in a tuberculosis sanitarium. (See the first of the fragments under *Cecilia.*)

We were to have had a final picture of Kathleen standing outside the studio. She has presumably separated from her husband as a result of the plot against Stahr. It had been one of her chief attractions for Stahr that she did not belong to the Hollywood world; and now she knows that she is never to be part of it. She is always to remain on the outside of things—a situation which also has its tragedy.

NOTES

CHAPTER I

The author has written at the top of his last draft of the first chapter, as given here:

Rewrite from mood. Has become stilted with rewriting. Don't look [at previous draft]. Rewrite from mood.

———

Page 20. Fitzgerald's first sketch for the end of the chapter perhaps conveys his idea more completely than he had succeeded in doing in this draft:

This will be based on a conversation that I had with ——— the first time I was alone with him in 1927, the day that he said a thing about railroads. As near as I can remember what he said was this:

We sat in the old commissary at ——— and he said, "Scottie, supposing there's got to be a road through a mountain—a railroad, and two or three surveyors and people come to you and you believe some of them and some of them you don't believe, but all in all, there seem to be half a dozen possible roads through those mountains, each one of which, so far as you can determine, is as good as the other. Now suppose you happen to be the top man, there's a point where you don't exercise the faculty of judgment in the ordinary way, but simply the faculty of arbitrary decision. You say, 'Well, I think we will put the road there,' and you trace it with your finger and you know in your secret heart, and no one else knows, that you have no reason for putting the road there rather than in several other different courses, but you're the only person that knows that you don't know why you're doing it and you've got to stick to that and you've got to pretend that you know and that you did it for specific reasons, even though you're utterly assailed by doubts

134

at times as to the wisdom of your decision, because all these other possible decisions keep echoing in your ear. But when you're planning a new enterprise on a grand scale, the people under you mustn't ever know or guess that you're in any doubt, because they've all got to have something to look up to and they mustn't ever dream that you're in doubt about any decision. Those things keep occurring."

At that point, some other people came into the commissary and sat down, and the first thing I knew there was a group of four and the intimacy of the conversation was broken, but I was very much impressed by the shrewdness of what he said—something more than shrewdness—by the largeness of what he thought and how he reached it at the age of twenty-six, which he was then.

So I think that this last episode will be when Stahr goes up and sits with the pilot up in front and rides beside the pilot, and the pilot recognizes in Stahr someone who in his own field must be just as sure, just as determined, just as courageous as he himself is. Very few words are exchanged between Stahr and the pilot—in fact, it is an episode that we may see entirely through the eyes of Cecilia peeping in, of the stewardess reporting to Cecilia what she saw peeping through the cockpit, or Schwartz still trying to get to Stahr before they get to Los Angeles. It is quite possible that we may not be alone with Stahr through this entire episode down to the very end, but at the very end I want to go into that strong feeling that I had in that undeveloped note about the motor shutting off and the plane settling down to earth and the lights of Los Angeles, and for a minute there, I want to give an all-fireworks illumination of the intense passion in Stahr's soul, his love of life, his love for the great thing that he's built out here, his, perhaps not exactly, satisfaction, but his feeling certainly of coming home to an empire of his own—an empire he has made.

I want to contrast this sharply with the feeling of those who have merely gypped another person's empire away from them like the four great railroad kings of the coast . . . or the feeling that —— would have. He's not interested in it because he owns it. He's interested in it as an artist because he has made it, and mixed up with his great feeling of triumph and happiness there must inevitably be a feeling of sadness with all acts of courage—a feeling that it is to some extent a finished thing, and doubt as to the next step as to how far he can go.

After the plane comes down, it may be best to finish the chapter with that fireworks—repeat my own fear when I landed in Los Angeles with the feeling of new worlds to conquer in 1937 transferred to Stahr, or it may be best to end with a cacophony of a rival.

CHAPTER II

Page 24. Fitzgerald had written Only fair *opposite the paragraph which begins,* "Robby'll take care of everything when he comes," Stahr assured Father. *This was to have been the first appearance of a character who was to play an important role, and the author wanted presumably, at this casual introduction, to give a sharper impression of him. His notes on Robinson will be found below among the preliminary sketches for the characters.*

CHAPTER III

This chapter had not been cut and organized to the author's complete satisfaction. It is given here as it stands in the manuscript, with only a few changes to make it self-consistent.

In the manuscript, the passage on page 46 reads as follows:

Probably the attack was planned, for Popolos, the Greek, took up the matter in a sort of double talk that reminded Prince Agge of Mike Van Dyke, except that it tried to be and succeeded in being clear instead of confusing.

The author had written a scene with which he was dissatisfied, in which the Prince had encountered Mike Van Dyke, the old gagman; but the double talk of Mike Van Dyke was intended to figure in some other place. The passages that deal with it follow:

"Hello, Mike," said Monroe. He introduced him to the visitor: "Prince Agge, this is Mr. Van Dyke. You've laughed at his stuff many times. He's the best gag-man in pictures."

"In the world," said the saucer-eyed man gravely, "—the funniest man in the world. How are you, Prince? . . ."

Immediately the Prince found himself engaged in conversation with Mike Van Dyke. He answered politely without quite getting the gist of his words. Something about the commissary, where Mr. Van Dyke thought he had seen the Prince trying to order what sounded like "twisted fish and a cat's handlebar," though the Prince was certain he misunderstood.

He tried to explain that he had not been to the commissary, but by this time they were so far into the subject that he thought the quickest way was to admit that he had, and merely parry Mr. Van Dyke's mistaken statements as to what he had done there. Mr. Van Dyke was not so much insistent as convinced, and he seemed to talk very fast. . . .

The Prince was introduced to Mr. Spurgeon and to Mr. and Mrs. Tarleton, but he was now so involved in the conversation with Mr. Van Dyke that he heard himself stammering, "I'm glad to meet me," because he was explaining to Van Dyke that he had *not* seen Technigarbo in Gretacolor. Again he had misunderstood. Was his name Albert Edward Butch Arthur Agge David, Prince of Denmark? "That's my cousin," he almost said, his head reeling.

Stahr's voice, clear and reassuring, brought him back to reality.

"That's enough, Mike.—That was 'double-talk'," he explained to Prince Agge. "It's considered funny here in the lower brackets. Do it slow, Mike."

Mike demonstrated politely.

"In an income at the gate this morning—" He pointed at Stahr. "—or did he?"

Baffled, the Dane bit again.

"What? Did he what?" Then he smiled: "I see. It is like your Gertrude Stein."

CHAPTER IV

Fitzgerald has the following note on the episode with the director at the beginning of this chapter:

What is missing in Ridingwood scene is passion and imagination, etc. What an extraordinary thing that it should all have been there for Ridingwood and then not there.

Page 97. After the words, And so he had learned tolerance, kindness, forbearance, and even affection like lessons, *the author has written for his own guidance*: (Now the idea about young and generous).

Note following the section that ends on page 98:

This may not be terse and clear enough here. Or perhaps I mean strong enough. It may be the place for the doctor's verdict. I would like to leave him on a stronger note.

TWO OUTLINES

The following letter and outline throw some light on the course of the story and show how it developed and changed from the author's first conception of it.

――――――

A letter written by Fitzgerald, September 29, 1939, explaining his original plans for the novel to his publisher and to the editor of a magazine in which he hoped to serialize it:

The story occurs during four or five months in the year 1935. It is told by Cecilia, the daughter of a producer named Bradogue in Hollywood. Cecilia is a pretty, modern girl, neither good nor bad, tremendously human. Her father is also an important character. A shrewd man, a gentile, and a scoundrel of the lowest variety. A self-made man, he has brought up Cecilia to be a princess, sent her East to college, made of her rather a snob, though, in the course of the story, her character evolves *away from this.* That is, she was twenty when the events that she tells occurred, but she is twenty-five when she tells about the events, and of course many of them appear to her in a different light.

Cecilia is the narrator because I think I know exactly how such a person would react to my story. She is *of* the movies but not *in* them. She probably was born the day *The Birth of a Nation* was previewed and Rudolf Valentino came to her fifth birthday party. So she is, all at once, intelligent, cynical, but understanding and kindly toward the people, great or small, who are of Hollywood.

She focuses our attention upon two principal characters—Milton Stahr and Thalia, the girl he loves.

In the beginning of the book I want to pour out my whole impression of this man Stahr as he is seen during an airplane trip from New York to the coast—of course, through Cecilia's eyes. She has been hopelessly in love with him for a long time. She is never going to win anything more from him than an affectionate regard, even that tainted by his dislike of her father.

Stahr is overworked and deathly tired, ruling with a radiance that is almost moribund in its phosphorescence. He has been warned that his health is undermined, but, being afraid of nothing, the warning is unheeded. He has had everything in life except the privilege of giving himself unselfishly to another human being. This he finds on the night of a semi-serious earthquake (like in 1935) a few days after the opening of the story.

It has been a very full day even for Stahr—the burst water mains, which cover the whole ground space of the lot to the depth of several feet, seem to release something in him. Called over to the outer lot to supervise the salvation of the electrical plant (for he has a finger in every pie of the vast bakery), he finds two women stranded on the roof of a property farmhouse and goes to their rescue.

Thalia Taylor is a twenty-six-year-old widow, and my present conception of her should make her the most glamorous and sympathetic of my heroines. Glamorous in a new way, because I am in secret agreement with the public in detesting the type of feminine arrogance that has been pushed into prominence in the case of ——, etc. People simply do not sympathize deeply with those who have had *all* the breaks, and I am going to dower this girl, like Rosalba in Thackeray's *Rose and the Ring,* with "a little misfortune." She and the woman with her (to whom she is serving as companion) have come secretly on the lot through the other woman's curiosity. They have been caught there when the catastrophe occurred.

Now we have a love affair between Stahr and Thalia, an immediate, dynamic, unusual, physical love affair—and I will write it so that you can publish it. At the same time I will send you a copy of how it will appear in book form somewhat stronger in tone.

This love affair is the meat of the book—though I am going to treat it, remember, as it comes through to Cecilia. That is to say by making Cecilia, at the moment of her telling the story, an intelligent and observant woman, I shall grant myself the privilege, as Conrad did, of letting her imagine the actions of the characters. Thus, I hope to get the verisimilitude of a first person narrative, combined with a Godlike knowledge of all events that happen to my characters.

Two events beside the love affair bulk large in the intermediary chapters. There is a definite plot on the part of Bradogue, Cecilia's father, to get Stahr out of the company. He has even actually and factually considered having him murdered. Bradogue is the monopolist at his worst—Stahr, in spite of the inevitable conservatism of the self-made man, is a paternalistic employer. Success came to him young, at twenty-three, and left certain idealisms of his youth unscarred. Moreover, he is a worker. Figuratively he takes off his coat and pitches in, while Bradogue is not interested in the making of pictures save as it will benefit his bank account.

The second incident is how young Cecilia herself, in her desperate love for Stahr, throws herself at his head. In her reaction at his indifference, she gives herself to a man whom she does not love. This episode is *not* absolutely necessary to the serial. It could be tempered, but it might be best to eliminate it altogether.

Back to the main theme: Stahr cannot bring himself to marry Thalia. It simply doesn't seem part of his life. He doesn't realize that she has become necessary to him. Previously his name has been associated with this or that well-known actress or society personality, and Thalia is poor, unfortunate, and tagged with a middle-class exterior which doesn't fit in with the grandeur Stahr demands of life. When she realizes this she leaves him temporarily, leaves him not because he has no legal intentions toward her but because of the hurt of it, the remainder of a vanity from which she had considered herself free.

Stahr is now plunged directly into the fight to keep control of the company. His health breaks down very suddenly while he is on a trip to New York to see the stockholders. He almost dies in New York and comes back to find that Bradogue has seized upon his absence to take steps which Stahr considers unthinkable. He plunges back into work again to straighten things out.

Now, realizing how much he needs Thalia, things are patched up between them. For a day or two they are ideally happy. They are going to marry, but he must make one more trip East to clinch the victory which he has conciliated in the affairs of the company.

Now occurs the final episode which should give the novel its quality—and its unusualness. Do you remember about 1933 when a transport plane was wrecked on a mountain-side in the Southwest, and a Senator was killed? The thing that struck me about it was that the country people rifled the bodies of the dead. That is just what happens to this plane which is bearing Stahr from Hollywood. The angle is that of three children who, on a Sunday picnic, are the first to discover the wreckage. Among those killed in the accident besides Stahr are two other characters we have met. (I have not been able to go into the minor characters in this short summary.) Of the three children, two boys and a girl, who find the bodies, one boy rifles Stahr's possessions; another, the body of a ruined ex-producer; and the girl, those of a moving picture actress. The possessions which the children find, symbolically determine their attitude toward their act of theft. The possessions of the moving picture actress tend the young girl to a selfish possessiveness; those of the unsuccessful producer sway one of the boys toward an irresolute attitude; while the boy who finds Stahr's briefcase is the one who, after a week, saves and redeems all three by going to a local judge and making full confession.

The story swings once more back to Hollywood for its finale. During the story *Thalia has never once been inside a studio.* After Stahr's death as she stands in front of the great plant which he created, she realizes now that she never will. She knows only that he loved her and that he was a great man and that he died for what he believed in. . . .

There's nothing that worries me in the novel, nothing that seems uncertain. Unlike *Tender is the Night,* it is not the story of deterioration—it is not depressing and not morbid in spite of the tragic ending. If one book could ever be "like" another, I should say it is more "like" *The Great Gatsby* than any other of my books. But I hope it will be entirely different—I hope it will be something new, arouse new emotions, perhaps even a new way of looking at certain phenomena. I have set it safely in a period of five years ago to obtain detachment, but now that Europe is tumbling about our ears this also seems to be for the best. It is an escape into a lavish, romantic past that perhaps will not come again into our time.

THIS DIAGRAM IS THE LAST OUTLINE MADE BY THE AUTHOR

	EPISODES			
A	June 28th 1. The plane. 2. Nashville. 3. Up forward. Different. 6000	Chapter (A) Introduce Cecilia, Stahr, White, Schwartz.	Act I June (The Plane) 6,000 STAHR	
B	July 28th 4. Johnny Swanson—Marcus leaving—Brady. 5. The earthquake. 6. The back lot. 3000	Chapter (B) Introduces Brady, Kathleen, Robinson and secretaries. Atmosphere of night—sustain.	Act II July—early August (The Circus) 21,000	
C	July 29th 7. The camera man. Stahr's work and health. From something she wrote. 8. First conference. 9. Second conference and afterwards. 10. Commissary and idealism about non-profit pictures. Rushes. Phone call, etc. 5000	Chapters (C & D) are equal to guest list and Gatsby's party. Throw everything into this, with selection. They must have a plot, though, leading to 13.		
D	11. Visit to rushes. 12. Second meeting that night. Wrong girl—glimpse. 2500		STAHR and KATHLEEN	
E	August 6th 13. Cecilia and Stahr and ball. 14. Malibu seduction. Try to get on lot. Dead middle. 15. Cecilia and father. 16. Phone call and wedding. 6000	Chapter (E) Three episodes. Atmosphere in 15 most important. Hint of Waste Land of the house too late.		

		Chapter	Act
F 17. The dam breaks with Brimmer.	August 10th	Chapter (F) This belongs to the women. It introduces Smith (for the first time?)	Act III August—early Sept. (The Underworld) 11,500
18. The cummerbund—market—(The theatre with Benchley).	August 20th		
19. The four meet. Renewal. Palomar.			
20. Wylie White in office.	5000		
G 21. Sick in Washington. To quit?	August 28th—Sept. 14th	Chapter (G) The blow falls on Stahr. Sense of heat all through, culminating in 25.	THE STRUGGLE
22. Brady and Stahr—double blackmail. Quarrel with Wylie.			
23. Throws over Cecilia, who tells her father. Stops making pictures. A story conference—rushes and sets. Lies low after cut.			
24. Last fling with Kathleen. Old stars in heat wave at Encino.	6500		
H 25. Brady gets to Smith. Fleishacker and Cecilia.	Sept. 15th-30th	Chapter (H) The suit and the price.	Act IV (The Murderers) 7,000
26. Stahr hears plan. Camera man O.K. Stops it—very sick.			
27. Resolve problem. Kathleen at airport; Cecilia to college.	7000		DEFEAT
I 28. The plane falls. Foretaste of the future in Fleishacker.	Sept. 30th—Oct.	Chapter (I) Stahr's death.	Act V October (The End) 4,500
29. Outside the studio.			EPILOGUE
30. Johnny Swanson at funeral.	4500		51,000

CECILIA

*The first of the following fragments was originally written to
stand as an introduction to the story; but Fitzgerald decided to discard it because he was afraid it would make the opening too depressing. The picture of Cecilia in the tuberculosis sanitarium was,
however, to appear at the end of the book.*

We two men were fascinated by that young face. A few months
ago, we had made a short trip to the canyons of the Colorado as if
for a last gape at life; now back at the hospital this girl's face in the
sunset, and with the fever, seemed to share some of the primordial
rose tints of that "natural wonder."

"Go on tell us," we said. "We don't know about such things."

She started to cough, changed her mind—as one can.

"I don't mind telling *you*. But why should our friends, the
asthmas, have to hear?"

"They're going," we assured her.

We three waited, our heads leant back on our chairs, while a
nurse marshalled a flustered little group that must have heard the
remark—and edged them toward the sanitarium. The nurse cast a
reproachful glance back at Cecilia as if she wanted to return and slap
her—but the glance changed its mind and the nurse hurried in after
her flock.

"They're gone. Now tell us."

Cecilia stared up at the brilliant Arizona sky. She regarded it—
the blue air, which to us had once stood for hope in the morning
—not with regret but rather with the cocksure confusion of those the
depression caught in mid-adolescence. Now she was twenty-five.

"Anything you want to know," she promised. "I don't owe *them*
any loyalty. Oh, they fly over and see me sometimes, but what do I
care—I'm ruined."

"We're all ruined," I said mildly.

She sat up, the Aztec figures of her dress emerging from the
Navajo pattern of her blanket. The dress was thin—gone native for
the sun country—and I remembered the round shining knobs of
another girl's shoulders at another time and place, but here we must
all stay in the shadow.

"You shouldn't talk like that," she assured me. "I'm ruined, but you're just two good guys who happened to get a bug."

"You don't grant us any history," we objected with senescent irony. "Nobody over forty is allowed a history."

"I didn't mean that. I mean you'll get *well*."

"In case we don't, tell us the story. You still hear this stuff about him. What was he: Christ in Industry? I know boys who worked on the Coast and hated his guts. Were you crazy about him? Loosen up, Cecilia. Something for a jaded palate! Think of the hospital dinner we'll face in half an hour."

Cecilia's glance suspected, then rejected our existence—not our right to live, but our right to any important feeling of loss or passion or hope or high excitement. She started to talk, waited for a tickle to subside in her throat.

"He never looked at me," she said indignantly, "and I won't talk about him when you're in this mood."

She threw off the blanket and stood up, her center-parted hair falling from her wan temples, ripples from a brown dam. She was high-breasted and emaciated, still perfectly the young woman of her time. Superiority was implicit in her heel taps as she walked through the open door into the corridor of the building—our only road to wonderland. Apparently Cecilia believed in nothing at present, but it seemed she had once known another road, passed by it a long time ago.

We were sure, nevertheless, that some time she would tell us about it—and so she did. What follows is our imperfect version of her story.

———

This is Cecilia taking up the story. I should probably explain why I spent so much of the summer hanging around the studio. Well, for one thing, I was too big to keep out now and I knew how to do it without bothering people. Secondly, I had had a difference with Wylie White about who had the say about my body, so there was a man named X whom I didn't intend to marry who was playing the man who *al*most got the girl in three pictures at once and had to be on the lot. And thirdly, most important, I had nothing else to do. (Fourth, with description of Hollywood boys.)

———

[*Cecilia and Kathleen*]

She wore a little summer number from Saks, about $18.98, and a pink and blue hat that had been stepped on on one side. Her nails were pale pink, almost natural, and her hair you couldn't be absolutely sure of. She was polite and rather overwhelmed. X spent some time trying to convey who I was, but kept bumping against the flat fact that Kathleen Moore had never heard of my father.

"I've been looking for a job," she said.

"What kind of a job?"

"I've been going through the advertisements. What is a swami?"

X explained—it was very interesting.

"He was the most encouraging," Kathleen said. "But I'm afraid it wouldn't do—that filthy towel about his head."

Father used to have great scraps with the Jews over Jewish and Irish tricks. The Jews claimed he always oversold his points. Father thought he was just right. For instance, [his] weeping trick.

STAHR

Stahr's day would begin often enough right in the studio. Since his wife's death, he frequently slept there; his suite contained a bath and dressing-room, and his divan made a bed. With the immense distances of Los Angeles County—three hours a day in an automobile is not exceptional—this was a great saving of time.

Never wanted his name on pictures—"I don't want my name on the screen because credit is something that should be given to others. If you are in a position to give credit to yourself, then you do not need it."

I want to tell also of his great failing of surrounding himself with men who were very far below him. However, this may have been because of a sureness about his health, because he felt in his 20's that he himself was able to keep a direct eye on everything, and, therefore, would have been hindered rather than helped by men who were positive-minded supervisors. His relation with directors, his importance in that he brought interference with their work to a minimum, and while he made enemies—and this is important—up to his arrival the director had been King Pin in pictures since Griffith made *The Birth of a Nation*. Now, therefore, some of the directors resented the fact that he reduced their position from one of complete king to being simply one element in a combine. His interest in the lot itself is important, his utter democracy, his popularity with the rank and file of the studio.

However, this is not really thinking out Stahr from the beginning. I must go back into his childhood and remember that remark of his mother: "We always knew that Monroe would be all right." . . . Remember also that he was a fighter even though he was a small man—certainly not more than 5′6½″, weighing very little (which is one reason he always liked to see people sitting down), and remember when the man tried to get fresh with his wife at Venice how he lost his temper and got into a fight. . . . He must have been a scrapper from early boyhood, probably a neighborhood scrapper. Remember also how popular he was with men from the beginning in a free and easy way, that is to say, as a man that liked to sit around with his feet up and smoke and "be one of the boys." He was essentially more of a man's man than a ladies' man.

There was never anything priggish or superior in his casual conversation that makes men uneasy in the company of other men. He used to run sometimes with a rather fast crowd of directors— many of them heavy drinkers, though he wasn't one himself. And they accepted him as one of themselves in a "hale fellow, well met" spirit—that is: in spite of the growing austerity which overwork forced on him in later years, Stahr never had any touch of the prig or the siss about him, and I think this was real and not an overlay. To that extent he was Napoleonic and actually liked combat—which leads me back to the supposition that probably he was a scrapper as a boy and had always been that way. If, after he came into full power, he sometimes resorted to subterfuge to have his way, that was the result of his position rather than anything in his nature. I think, by nature, he was very direct, frank, challenging. Try to analyze what his probable boyhood was from the above.

This chapter must not develop into merely a piece of character

analysis. Each statement that I make about him must contain at the
end of every few hundred words some pointed anecdote or story to
keep it alive. I do not want it to have the ring of an analysis. I
want it to have as much drama throughout as the story of old
Laemmle himself on the telephone.

———————

Stahr knew he had a working knowledge of technics, but because
he had been head man for so long and so many apprentices had
grown up during his sway, more knowledge was attributed to him
than he possessed. He accepted this as the easiest way and was an
adept though cautious bluffer. In the dubbing-room, which was for
sound what the cutting-room was for sight, he worked by ear
alone and was often lost amid the chorus of ever newer terms and
slang. So on the stops. He watched the new processes of faking
animated backgrounds, moving pictures taken against the background of other moving pictures, with a secret child's approval.
He could have understood easily enough—often he preferred not
to, to preserve a sensual acceptance when he saw the scene unfold
in the rushes. There were smart young men about—Reinmund was
one—who phrased their remarks to convey the impression that they
understood everything about pictures. Not Stahr. When he interfered, it was always from his own point of view, not from theirs.
Thus his function was different from that of Griffith in the early
days, who had been all things to every finished frame of film.

———————

It is doubtful if any of these head men read through a single
work of the imagination in a year. And Stahr, who had no time
whatever to read and must depend on synopses, began to doubt that
any of his supervisors read more than what was ordered; he doubted
that his casting people (note for a character here) covered the range
he would have wanted them to. A show played a year and a half
in San Francisco—the specialty in it was discovered only after it
reached Los Angeles, where young teats drew a tired sabled audience,
and the specialty was in a boom market within a week. And had to
be paid for against important budgets where alertness would have
bought it for nothing.

———————

In order to forgive Stahr for what he did that afternoon, it should be remembered that he came out of the old Hollywood that was rough and tough and where the wildest bluffs hold. He had manufactured gloss and polish and control of the new Hollywood, but occasionally he liked to tear it apart just to see if it was there.

But now as he stood there and the orchestra began to play and the dancers stood up, a sentence spoke in his mind that surprised him: "I am bored beyond measure," it said.

Even the words did not sound like him. "Beyond measure" was theatrical, he wondered if he had read it recently. He did not go out often enough to be bored or to think of it like that. He knew how to elude bores, and he had grown to accept deference and admiration as something to wear with humility and grace; and he almost always had a good time.

Some men came up to him, and he talked to them with his hands in his pockets. One was an agent who hated him and always referred to him, so Stahr was told, as "The Vine Street Jesus," "The Walking Oscar," or "The Back-to-Use Napoleon."

At some point after censorship, Monroe revolts against childishness.

Show Stahr hiding in retreat or avoiding people without hurting them.

Like many men, he did not like flowers except a few weedy ones —they were too highly evolved and self-conscious. But he liked leaves and peeled twigs, horse chestnuts and even acorns, unripe, ripe and wormy fruit.

Stahr is miserable and embittered toward the end.

Before death, thoughts from *Crack-Up*.
Do I look like death? (in mirror at 6 P.M.)

Men who have been endowed with unusual powers for work or analysis or ingredients that go to make big personal successes, seem to forget as soon as they are rich that such abilities are not evenly distributed among the men of their kind. So when the suggestion of a Union springs out of this act of Bradogue's [Brady's], Stahr seems to reverse his form, join the other side and almost to ally himself with Bradogue. Note also in the epilogue that I want to show that Stahr left certain harm behind him just as he left good behind him. That some of his reactionary creations such as the Screen Playwrights existed long after his death just as so much of his valuable creative work survived him. However, remember this is to play a small part in this chapter and must be written epigrammatically, cleverly and perhaps placed in the mouth of one whom we may see leaving Hollywood in this chapter [the final departure of Stahr in the plane]. In any case, it must not be allowed to interfere with the mood of this short chapter, which would, whether treated in a close-up or remotely, belong to Thalia [Kathleen] and leave Thalia to linger in the reader's mind.

KATHLEEN

The realization came to her that the tracks of life would never lead anywhere and were like tracks of the airplane; that no one knew of their place, since there was no Daniel Boone to hack trees; that the world had to go on and that it wasn't going to be inside her and there still had to be those tracks. It was an awful lonesome journey.

———

She thought of electric fans in little restaurants with lobsters on ice in the windows, and of pearly signs glittering and revolving against the obscure, urban sky, the hot, dark sky. And pervading everything, a terribly strange, brooding mystery of roof tops and empty apartments, of white dresses in the paths of parks, and fingers for stars and faces instead of moons, and people with strange people scarcely knowing one another's names.

———

Bright unused beauty still plagued her in the mirror.

[Kathleen and her husband?]

He found her in the cabin, just standing, thinking. He was afraid of her when she thought, knowing that in the part of her most removed from him, there was taking place a tireless ratiocination, the synthesis of which has always a calm sense of the injustice and unsatisfactions of life. He knew the [?] with which her mind worked, but he was always surprised that it brought forth in the end protests that were purely abstract, and in which he figured only as an element as driven and succorless as herself. This made him more afraid than if she said, "It was your fault," as she frequently did—for by it she seemed to lift the situation and its interpretation out of his grasp. In that region his mind was more feminine than hers—he felt light, and off his balance—and a little like the Dickens character who accused his wife of praying against him.

STAHR AND KATHLEEN

Object: I wanted a seduction—very Californian, yet new—very Hollywood, say. If he has no illusion, he has at least great pity and excitement, friendliness, stimulus, fascination.

Where will the warmth come from in this? Why does he think she's warm? Warmer than the voice in *Farewell to Arms*. My girls were all so warm and full of promise. What can I do to make it honest and different?

The sea at night. Como. St.-Pol (used in *Tender*). Why are French romances cold and sad *au fond?*—why was Wells warm?

General Mood. Shaken by the flare-up, they go back, she still thinking she can withdraw. She could not bear to think. It was tonight. It is a murky, rainy dusk, a dreary day (change former time to sunset). They left the hotel a little more than three hours ago, but it seemed a long time. Get them there quickly. Odd effect of the place like a set. The mood should be two people—free. He has an overwhelming urge toward the girl, who promises to give life back to him—though he has no idea yet of marriage—she is the heart of hope and freshness. *He seduces her because she is slipping away—* she lets herself be seduced because of overwhelming admiration (the phone call). Once settled, it is sensual, breathless, immediate, then gentle and tender for awhile.

She was very ready and it was right. It would have been good any time, but for the first time it was much more than he had hoped or expected. Not like very young people, but wise and fond and chokingly sweet, as it had been with Minna when sometimes they had gone for many days. He was away for a hundred miles for a visit to himself, but he did not let her see.

This girl had a life—it was very seldom he met anyone whose life did not depend in some way on him or hope to depend on him.

ROBINSON

These passages about Robinson all relate to an earlier plan for the story. The author had discarded his original idea of having Kathleen have a love affair with Robinson, but the latter was perhaps still to figure as the agent selected by Brady to put Stahr out of the way. Kathleen is here called Thalia.

I would like this episode to give a picture of the work of a cutter, camera man or second unit director in the making of such a thing as *Winter Carnival,* accenting the speed with which Robinson works, his reactions, why he is what he is instead of being the very high-salaried man which his technical abilities entitle him to be. I might as well use some of the Dartmouth atmosphere, snow, etc., being careful not to impinge at all on any material that Walter Wanger may be using in *Winter Carnival* or that I may have ever suggested as material to him.

I could begin the chapter through Cecilia's eyes, who is a guest at the carnival, skip quickly to Robinson and have them perhaps meet at a telegraph desk where she sees him sending a wire to Thalia. But by this time and through the material I choose—photographing backgrounds for the snow picture—I should not only develop the character of Robinson as he is, but leave a loophole showing the possibility of his being later corrupted. In a very short transition or montage, I bring the whole party West on the Chief. Cecilia, perhaps with friends of her own, coaxes the producer who has been in charge (ineffectual producer) and Robinson.

The man chosen tentatively to put Stahr out of the way is Robinson the cutter. Must develop Robinson character so that this is possible—that is, Robinson now has three aspects. His top possibility as a sort of Sergeant———character as planned. His relation with the world, which is conventional and rather stereotyped and trite; and this new element, in which it would be possible for him to be so corrupted by circumstances as to be drawn into such a matter and used by Bradogue. To do this it is practically necessary that there must be from the beginning some flaw in Robinson in spite of his courage, his resourcefulness, his technical expertness and the Sergeant ———virtues I intend to give him. Some secret flaw—perhaps something sexual. It might be possible, but if I do that, then he could have had no relation with Thalia, who certainly would not have accepted a bad lover. Perhaps he would have some flaw, not sexual—not unmanly—in any case have no special idea at present, and this must be invented. In any case, his having loved Thalia would make him a very natural tool for Bradogue to use in playing on his natural jealousy of Stahr.

———

[Thalia] has been having an affair intermittently, of which she is half ashamed, with the character whom I have called Robinson, the cutter, who is in his (and this is very important) professional life an extraordinarily interesting and subtle character on the idea of Sergeant———in the army or that cutter at United Artists whom I so admired or any other person of the type of trouble shooter or film technician—and I want to contrast this sharply with his utter conventionality and acceptance of banalities in the face of what might be called the cultural urban world. Women can twist him around their little finger. He might be able to unravel the most twisted skein of wires in a blinding snowstorm on top of a sixty-foot telephone pole in the dark with no more tools than an imperfect pair of pliers made out of the nails of his boots, but faced with the situation which the most ignorant and useless person would handle with urbanity he would seem helpless and gawky—so much so as to give the impression of being a Babbitt or of being a stupid, gawky, inept fellow.

This contrast at some point in the story is recognized by Stahr, who must at all points, when possible, be pointed up as a man who sees below the surface into reality.

Her attitude towards this man has been that even in the niceties of love-making she has had to be his master, and his deep gratitude to her is allied to his love for her, though throughout the story he always feels that she is inevitably the superior person. Stahr at some point points it out to her that this is nonsense and I want to show here something different in men's and women's points of view: particularly that women are prone to cling to an advantage or rather have less human generosity in points of character than men have, or do I mean a less wide point of view?

Stahr nodded and walked along at the head of his gang. Robinson, who was almost beside him, but a little behind, was a hard-jawed technician—supposed to be the best cutter in Hollywood. I didn't come in contact with that class, but I know Robinson was such a good cutter that often he had been asked to direct a picture. He had tried once, back in the silent days, and it was a failure. Never, never would a man like Jack Robinson want to steer a venture, if I know what I'm talking about. From the time he was called from his job on top of telephone posts in Michigan thunderstorms to the intricate task of trying, as a sergeant, to establish tangible liaison with the artillery in his infantry division. At that point when he found that an uneducated trouble-shooter was worth a dozen hit-or-miss shave-tails, called "signal officers," he had lost faith in his superiors and never afterward wanted to be anything except a liaison between what was commanded from above and what could be done below.

There was something warm about him that Stahr liked. Often he would edge up to Stahr, sensing the truth or falsity in some story—but in practice his advice faded to, "Oh, what the hell— what do these ——s know? All right. Go on. Where do we run these wires? *Sure*, it's a great idea."

CRASH OF THE PLANE

Fitzgerald had sketched in some detail the episode of the children finding the fallen plane, which is mentioned in the letter to his publisher. He had at one point decided to discard this, as he thought that the account of Stahr's funeral would make a better epilogue; but a note evidently written at a later time shows that he was still considering it.

It is important that I begin this chapter with a delicate transition, because I am not going to describe the fall of the plane, but simply give a last picture of Stahr as the plane takes off, and describe very briefly in the airport the people who are on board. The plane, therefore, has left for New York, and when the reader turns to Chapter X, I must be sure that he isn't confused by the sudden change of scene and situation. Here I can make the best transition by an opening paragraph in which I tell the reader that Cecilia's story ends here and that what is now told was a situation discovered by the writer himself and pieced together from what he learned in a small town in Oklahoma, from a municipal judge. That the incidents occurred one month after the plane fell and plunged Stahr and all its occupants into a white darkness. Tell how the snow hid the wreck and that in spite of searching parties the plane was considered lost, and then will resume the narrative—that a curtain first went up during an early thaw the following March. (I have to go over all the chapters and get the time element to shape up so that Stahr's second trip to New York, the one on which he is killed, takes place when the first snow has fallen on the Rockies. I want this plane to be like that plane that was lost for fully two months before they found the plane and the survivors.) Consider carefully whether if possible by some technical trick it might not be advisable to conceal from the reader that the plane fell until the moment when the children find it. The problem is that the reader must not turn to Chapter X and be confused, but, on the other hand, the dramatic effect, even if the reader felt lost for a few minutes, might be more effective if he did not find at the beginning of the chapter that the plane fell. In fact, almost certainly that is the way to handle it, and I must find a method of handling it in that fashion. There must be an intervening paragraph to begin Chapter X which will reassure the reader that he is following the same story, but it can be evasive and confine itself to leading the reader astray thinking that the paragraph is merely to explain that Cecilia is not telling this next part of the story without telling the reader that the plane ran into a mountain top and disappeared from human knowledge for several months.

When I have given the reader some sense of the transition and prepared him for a change in scene and situation, break the narrative with a space or so and begin the following story. That a group of children are starting off on a hike. That there is an early spring thaw in this mountain state. Pick out of the group of children, three whom we will call Jim, Frances, and Dan. That atmosphere is that particular atmosphere of Oklahoma when the long winter breaks. The atmosphere must be an all-cold climate where the winter breaks very suddenly with almost a violence—the snow seems to part as if very unwillingly in great convulsive movements like the break-up of an ice floe. There's a bright sun. The three children get separated from the teacher or scoutmaster or whoever is in charge of the expedition, and the girl, Frances, comes upon a part of the engine and fly-wheel of a broken airplane. She has no idea what it is. She is rather puzzled by it and at the moment is engaged rather in a flirtation with both Jim and Dan. However, she is an intelligent child of thirteen or fourteen and while she doesn't identify it as part of an airplane, she knows it is an odd piece of machinery to be found in the mountains. First she thinks it is the remains of some particular mining machinery. She calls Dan and then Jim, and they forget whatever small juvenile intrigue they were embarking on in their discovery of other debris from the fall of the plane. Their first general instinct is to call the other members of the party, because Jim, who is the smartest of the children (both the boys' ages about fifteen), recognizes that it is a fallen plane—though he doesn't connect it with the plane that disappeared the previous November—when Frances comes upon a purse and an open travelling case which belonged to the actress. It contains the things that to her represent undreamt of luxuries. In it there's a jewel box. It has been unharmed—it has fallen through the branches of a tree. There are flasks of perfume that would never appear in the town where she lives, perhaps a negligee or anything

I can think of that an actress might be carrying which was absolutely the last word in film elegance. She is utterly fascinated.

Simultaneously Jim has found Stahr's briefcase—a briefcase is what he has always wanted, and Stahr's briefcase is an excellent piece of leather—and some other travelling appurtenances of Stahr's. Things that are notably possessions of wealthy men. I have no special ideas at present, but think what a very wealthy, well-equipped man might be liable to have with him on such an expedition and then Dan makes the suggestion of "Why do we have to tell about this? We can all come up here later, and there is probably a lot more of this stuff here, and there's probably money and everything—these people are dead, they will never need it again—then we can say about the plane or let other people find it. Nobody will know we have been up here."

Dan bears, in some form of speech, a faint resemblance to Bradogue. This must be subtly done and not look too much like a parable or moral lesson, still the impression must be conveyed, but be careful to convey it once and not rub it in. If the reader misses it, let it go—don't repeat. Show Frances as malleable and amoral in the situation, but show a definite doubt on Jim's part, even from the first, as to whether this is fair dealing even towards the dead. Close this episode with the children rejoining the party.

Several weeks later the children have now made several trips to the mountain and have rifled the place of everything that is of any value. Dan is especially proud of his find, which includes some rather disreputable possessions of Ronciman. Frances is worried and definitely afraid and tending to side with Jim, who is now in an absolutely wretched mood about the whole affair. He knows that searching parties have been on a neighboring mountain—that the plane has been traced and that with the full flowering of spring the secret will come out and that each trip up he feels that the danger is more and more. However, let that be Frances' feeling, because Jim has, by this time, read the contents of Stahr's briefcase and late at night, taking it from the woodshed where he has concealed it, has gotten an admiration for the man. Naturally, by the time of this episode all three children are aware of what plane it was and who was in it and whose possessions they have.

One day also they have found the bodies, though I do not want

to go into this scene in any gruesome manner, of the six or seven
victims still half concealed by the snow. In any case, something in
one of Stahr's letters that Jim reads late at night decides him to go to
Judge ———— and tell the whole story, which he does against the
threats of Dan, who is bigger than he is and could lick him physically. We leave the children there with the idea that they are in
good hands, that they are not going to be punished, that they have
made full restoration, and the fact that, after all, they could plead
in court that they did not know anything more about the situation
than "finders keepers." There will be no punishment of any kind
for any of the three children. Give the impression that Jim is all
right—that Frances is faintly corrupted and may possibly go off in
a year or so in search of adventure and may turn into anything from
a gold digger to a prostitute, and that Dan has been completely corrupted and will spend the rest of his life looking for a chance to get
something for nothing.

I cannot be too careful not to rub this in or give it the substance
or feeling of a moral tale. I should [show] very pointedly that Jim
is all right and end perhaps with Frances and let the readers hope
that Frances is going to be all right and then take that hope away
by showing the last glimpse of Frances with that lingering conviction
that luxury is over the next valley, therefore giving a bitter and acrid
finish to the incident to take away any possible sentimental and
moral stuff that may have crept into it. Certainly end the incident
with Frances.

————————

Effect on children idea persists. Plane might fall in suburb of Los
Angeles. He thinks it was hills, but it's right there—a desolation
he helped to create.

HOLLYWOOD, ETC.

It is impossible to tell you anything of Stahr's day except at the
risk of being dull. People in the East pretend to be interested in how
pictures are made, but if you actually tell them anything, you find
they are only interested in Colbert's clothes or Gable's private life.
They never see the ventriloquist for the doll. Even the intellectuals,

who ought to know better, like to hear about the pretensions, extravagances and vulgarities—tell them pictures have a private grammar, like politics or automobile production or society, and watch the blank look come into their faces.

I could try, for instance, to make you understand what Stahr meant by his peculiar use of the word "nice," something like what Saint-Simon meant by *la politesse,* and you would classify what I had said as a lecture on taste.

The Warner Brothers narrative writing and the Metro dramatic, packed—cut back and forth writing from Stahr.

[*Stahr and Prince Agge*]

"Come on: we'll go get some lunch." Casually he added: "Broaca is the best man in Hollywood except Lubitsch and Vidor. But he's getting old and it makes him cross. He doesn't see that a director isn't everything in pictures now. That comes from the days when they shot off the cuff."

"The cuff?"

They started out the door. Stahr laughed.

"The director was supposed to have the plot on his cuff. There wasn't any script. Writers were all called gag-men—usually reporters and all souses. They stood behind the director and made suggestions, and if he liked it and it fitted with what was on his cuff, he staged it and took his footage."

The situation on the big lot was that every producer, director and scenarist there could adduce proof that he was a money-maker. With the initial distrust of the industry by business, with the weeding out of better men from the needs of speed, with the emphasis as in a mining camp on the lower virtues; then with the growing complication of technique and the elusiveness it created—it could fairly be said of all and by all of those who remained that they had made money—despite the fact that not a third of the producers or one-twentieth of the writers could have earned their living in the East. There was not one of these men, no matter how low-grade or incompetent a fellow, who could not claim to have participated largely in success. This made difficulty in dealing with them.

Remember my summing-up in *Crazy Sunday*—don't give the impression that these are bad people.

Actress—introduced so slowly, so close, so real that you believe in her. Somehow she's first sitting next to you, not an actress but with all the qualifications, loud and dissonant in your ear. Then she *is* one, but don't let it drift away in detailed description of her career. Keep her close. Never iust use her name. Always begin with a mannerism.

The Beard. Monty Woolley's beard. 50 peddle the muff. Family supported by beard. It hasn't worked for seven weeks. It was wonderful in *Hurricane*. It got a poor deal Wednesday. For a gag going to cut it off—work I lose. How much prestige, *amour propre*. Damage to ego. $30,000. Fake beard cut off.

Tillie Losch worried about what "exotic" meant.

He was so new as a scenarist that when the agent came in, he thought he wanted him to write something for the paper. [This refers to the habit of the Hollywood trade papers of shaking down new-comers for ads under threat of giving them bad publicity or none.]

Man [from Hollywood trade paper] advising me not to read the book.

Character of X, *poor* producer.
—— saying afterwards that he died with silent pictures.
We need a new formula.

The cleverly expressed opposite of any generally accepted idea is worth a fortune to somebody.

Joke about "Shoot it both ways."

___

"We could tap out something," she said—as a colored maid says, "I'll rinse out your stockings," to minimize the work.

___

Great masses of wires on floor—can hear everyone through dictophone.

___

Her ash-blond hair seemed weather-proof save for a tiny curtain of a bang that was evidently permitted, even expected, to stir a little in a mild wind. She had an unmistakable aura about her person of being carefully planned. Under minute scallops that were scarcely brows, her eyes, etc. Her teeth were so white against the tan, her lips so red, that in combination with the blue of her eyes, the effect was momentarily startling—as startling as if the lips had been green and the pupils white.

___

She feared the black cone hanging from the metal arm, shrilling and shrilling across the sunny room. It stopped for a minute, replaced by her heartbeats; then began again.

___

Hollywood child. The little hard face of a successful street-walker on a jumping-jack's body, the clear cultured whine of the voice.

___

Most of us could be photographed from the day of our birth to the day of our death and the film shown, without producing any emotion except boredom and disgust. It would all just look like monkeys scratching. How do you feel about your friends' home movies about their baby or their trip? Isn't it a godawful bore?

___

A football team on a blazing hot July day. Two hot teams mousing around at $500 a day. Actors, extras and a camera crew. High in the empty stadium, Stahr and his girl.

___

There was, for example, a man who in all seriousness asked him this favor: Stahr was to say, "Hello, Tim," and slap him on the back in front of the commissary one morning. Stahr had the man's record traced, and then slapped him on the back. The man ascended into Heaven.

Almost literally, for he was taken into one of the best agencies— which is what George Gershwin referred to when he said, "It's nice work if you can get it." He sits there today, with a picture of his wife and children on the wall, and has his nails manicured at the Beverly Hills Hotel. His life is one long happy dream.

Stahr remembered how they had used the three freaks back in 1927. X was being bothered by a really appalling woman. The day before the case came to trial, he sent a dwarf and [two other freaks] to her with messages. His counsel opened by stating that the woman was crazy. On the stand she told about her visitors—the jury shook their heads, winked at each other and acquitted.

Cecilia's uncle is an idiot like ———'s brother.

"—the rugged individualism of Tommy Manville, Barbara Hutton and Woolie Donahue." Never forgiven Wylie for slipping it into his speech when he was supporting Landon.

There is a place for a hint somewhere of a big agent, to complete the picture.

A tall round-shouldered young man with a beaked nose and soft brown eyes in a sensitive face.

The awful reverberating thunder of his absence.

[*Airplane Trip*]

My blue dream of being in a basket like a kite held by a rope against the wind.

It's fun to stretch and see the blue heavens spreading once more, spreading azure thighs for adventure.

Girl like a record with a blank on the other side.

There are no second acts in American lives.

Tragedy of these men was that nothing in their lives had really bitten deep at all.

Bald Hemingway characters.

---

wily plagiarist
exigent overlordship
not one survived the castration

Don't wake the Tarkington ghosts.

ACTION IS CHARACTER.